Raffia - Text copyright © Emmy Ellis 2025
Cover Art by Emmy Ellis @ studioenp.com © 2025

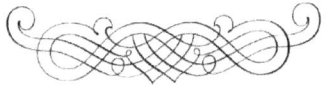

All Rights Reserved

Raffia is a work of fiction. All characters, places, and events are from the author's imagination. Any resemblance to persons, living or dead, events or places is purely coincidental.

The author respectfully recognises the use of any and all trademarks.

With the exception of quotes used in reviews, this book may not be reproduced or used in whole or in part by any means existing without written permission from the author.

Warning: The unauthorised reproduction or distribution of this copyrighted work is illegal. No part of this book may be scanned, uploaded, or distributed via the Internet or any other means, electronic or print, without the author's written permission. The author does not give permission for any part of this book to be used in AI.

Published by Five Pyramids Press, Suite 1a 34 West Street,
Retford, England, DN22 6ES
ISBN: 9798288280108

RAFFIA

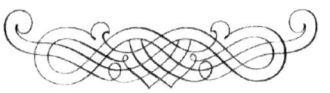

Emmy Ellis

Chapter One

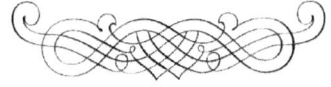

Freya Duncan couldn't stand paying for the ridiculously overpriced stuff in the hotel shop any longer. Thirty US dollars for sun cream? Thirteen for a packet of crisps or ten for a bag of Haribo? It was so obvious holidaymakers were being taken for mugs, and there wasn't much anyone could do about it unless they wanted to venture off the resort to the

supermarket a thirty-minute walk away. She could go in one of the taxis constantly parked outside the hotel, she supposed, but the men in casual clothing waiting to pounce the second anyone looked like they were leaving—it put her off. She'd rather use Uber. At least that way there was a record of her going with someone.

She'd read the reviews about the place before she'd booked her trip. People had advised not to leave the resort because of the touting from locals. Others had said a simple "no thank you" sufficed and you were left alone. Signs around the hotel warned guests not to engage in any transactions with anyone other than the spa staff or those in the "boutique" (namely the overpriced shop).

Jamaica had been a dream destination for such a long time, but sadly, Freya's view of it had changed once she'd seen it for herself, up close and personal. Every picture she'd seen, every representation on TV had given the impression it was a place of luxury. Hadn't her friend, Lottie, recently used the word "exotic" when Freya had met her for a coffee to chat about where she was going and why? But on the way from the airport to the resort, she'd stared out of the coach window, presented with such obvious poverty she'd felt sad for the people trying to survive.

In between magnificent houses, shacks appeared out of place. People sat on the roadside behind wonky tables selling fruit. Others swept dusty yards, and when a sudden bout of rain had poured, they'd either continued their work or ran to hide beneath corrugated-iron overhangs. Clothing was minimal—totally understandable in the humid heat—but what they did have on was worn or looked old.

She was ashamed of her pretty summer dresses packed in her suitcase. Ashamed of spending two weeks sunbathing at an all-inclusive. She remembered something someone on the coach had said when her partner had commented on the sight out of the window: "They need tourism, so if we didn't come…" Freya had felt a little better to think she was helping people to earn a living, especially when she'd used Google to check how much the resort staff got paid per year.

Utterly shocking. From then on, she'd given tips to anyone who served her.

Earlier this morning, she'd visited the holiday rep in the foyer before embarking on her trip to the supermarket. Assured that it was safe outside the grounds, Freya set off up the long driveway lined with palm trees and bushes; the rep had said it took fifteen minutes to walk up it, then another fifteen to the shops.

The heat was too much today, but she'd put cream on, so hopefully she wouldn't burn, then she could come back and sit by the pool in the shade of a parasol.

She passed the splash park on the left, part of the resort, and smiled to herself at the shrieks from kids on the large multicoloured tube slides, then the whoosh of water when they were unceremoniously dumped out of the ends. Farther on, she passed a row of white taxis. One of the drivers got out, approaching her. He seemed legit in his uniform of black trousers and a white shirt, and the shiny cabs had the same logo on the sides, nothing like the ones outside the hotel. He held up a business card and stopped in front of her, blocking her path. She couldn't decide whether he was menacing or not. His size and height intimidated her.

"Wagwan," he said.

"Um, wagwan," she said. "I don't need a taxi, thank you."

"Where are you going?" he asked.

"To the supermarket just down the road."

"You should let me take you…"

She shook her head.

"Or I could take you to Negril," he suggested.

"But I don't want to go there."

"Two hundred and fifty dollars."

She'd quickly realised which dollars people meant around here. Jamaican currency sounded so much higher—a thousand was around a fiver in the UK, so there was no way he was offering to take her to Negril for less than that, not all those miles away, so this price was US.

"There are lots of nice places to go to there," he went on. "Three hundred and fifty dollars."

"You just said it was two-fifty."

"No I didn't, I said three."

She didn't like the way he made her feel stupid, the way she was now doubting her hearing, but no, she'd definitely heard him right the first time.

He persisted. "Or I could take you to Dunn's River, that's not far. You can't come to Jamaica and not go there or see the other sites."

She bloody could!

Freya glanced at the other drivers in the line of taxis. Were they the same as him? If they got out to speak to her, would they try to pressure her, too? Much as she loved the resort, she'd quickly got pissed off with being approached by the spa ladies every morning as soon as she'd stepped off the lift. She didn't want a massage or her eyebrows done, nor did she want her hair cut. She just wanted to enjoy her holiday by herself, some space to tend to her broken heart.

"I only want to go to the supermarket!" She'd sounded rude and felt guilty, but God.

She skirted around him, hurrying up the driveway path. Once she'd got a sufficient distance away from him, she peered back. He'd gone into a little white building behind the splash park. Was that an office? Was it for the hotel's official taxi drivers?

She jumped as a bird shot straight in front of her. There were so many of them here and reminded her of the blackbirds from home, except these ones trilled a noise that sounded like an iPhone alarm going off. It had taken her a while to realise it was birds and not phones when she'd been by the pool on her first full day, and of course she'd googled it. Another bird that fascinated her resembled the Batman logo if she viewed it while lying on a sunbed and looking up at them in flight. At first she'd thought they were cormorants.

She walked on and, coming to the end of the driveway, frowned. On the way in on the coach, she'd been sitting on the right-hand side so had naturally looked out of that window, which meant she hadn't spotted the little hut with guards in beige uniforms standing in front of it. There were also gates to shut the resort off, something else she hadn't clocked. Why would the resort need gates and guards when the rep had told her it was safe here?

Should she change her mind about going to the supermarket? The sun cream at the boutique was thirty dollars yesterday and thirty-two today, and the little shop down the beach wasn't that much cheaper. She imagined it would be about ten in the supermarket, so yes, it was worth going.

The guards parted to reveal a table. On top, a ledger listed names, room numbers, and times.

"Where are you going?" the woman asked. No wagwan greeting from her, then. She didn't look too happy. Maybe she was hot and bothered.

"The supermarket." Freya glanced at the young male guard who smiled back at her and nodded.

"Sign out in the book," he said.

Freya did that, then checked the time on her phone so she could add it to the correct column. She supposed it was a good thing that there was a record of her leaving the resort. People could get lost in the jungle-like areas, although she wasn't daft enough to venture there on her own.

The woman flapped a hand for her to leave the resort. Three or four paces past the hut, and Freya almost turned around and ran back. A Jamaican man of about fifty pushed himself off of an ornate lamppost situated on a patch of grass in front of bushes that separated the resort grounds from what lay behind them. The hems of his black shorts rested just above his knobbly knees on extra-skinny legs. His mustard-coloured football shirt was tatty with loose threads from where the fabric had snagged. His hair clumped together in places where he hadn't taken care of it, and his fast-parting lips revealed only four front teeth at the top, broken and small and the colour so close to that of his gums it appeared he had no teeth at all. He walked closer. One leg bent inwards at the knee, as if he'd had a break at some point and his bones hadn't been set properly. Ragged black trainers covered his long feet.

She prepared herself to say no thank you to whatever he was about to offer. The poor bastard was clearly down on his luck, but she didn't need another braided bracelet or whatever he might be selling. If he was anything like the two men at the end of the beach who stood behind a waist-high wall with their goods propped on top of it, he'd probably offer her cups made out of bamboo, or carved plaques, or lots of painted turtles made out of wood.

Those men had introduced themselves as Cheap Fred and Cheap Pete. Those were so obviously not their names, and she'd known straight off the bat they were the looky-looky men of the area. Fred had been lovely to her, such a kind and gentle man, and she'd bought one of his bamboo cups. Peter had been pushy, trying to get her to buy a turtle, and because they were situated so far along from the private part of the beach belonging to the resort, she'd been uneasy with the pressure, so she'd paid Fred and rushed away.

"Wagwan," this new man said. "Do you need a taxi? Mine's just over there."

She glanced to where he indicated but couldn't see a car, only a pale-yellow building across the road, a washing line strung from it to a nearby tree, clothes flapping in the breeze that had been present since she'd arrived, something to be grateful for, considering it was so hot.

"No thank you, I'm going to walk."

"Let me just point you to where the shop is," he said, gesturing for her to follow him off the grass and around the edge of the bush.

Freya looked back at the guards who didn't seem fazed by this man at all. Maybe if she just let him point then he'd go away. She stepped out beside the bush and stared down the road, pleased there was a lot of traffic. People leaned on their horns a lot here, and yes, she'd searched Google to find out why. Apparently, as well as the usual reasons, the horn was used to say hello. Going by the amount of toots, everyone seemed to know everyone.

Behind the bush stood a squat white building with no windows, just empty squares. Seeing that compared to the lushness of the hotel once again brought home the differences between the haves and have nots. Her privilege stood out a mile, and even though she worked hard for her money and had done for years, a prickle of guilt still stabbed into her.

The man stopped to wait for her. "The name's Cool Raffia."

One thing she'd take back from this trip was that many people didn't just have one name. One of the bingo callers had introduced herself as Beautiful Barbie, another was Daring Delroy.

She looked at Cool Raffia's gummy smile and gave him a smile back, although she wasn't going to tell him her name. He turned to the side and pointed down the road. In the distance, on the right, stood a tall building that she hoped was the supermarket. Before that, homes on both sides interspersed with scrubland, random trees, and a few shrubs. Despite the flow of traffic, it felt somewhat desolate all the same.

"The supermarket is just down there," Cool Raffia said. "I'll show you."

"No, no, it's okay, you don't need to do that." Having seen the building ahead, she judged it wasn't

that far to the shop and could comfortably get there and back without a chaperone.

"It's fine, I want to help," he said, walking off.

"Is it dangerous around here or something?"

"No, it's safe. Very low crime rate."

So why did he feel the need to escort her?

She'd read about how you had to be careful in some places, like if you took hold of something that was being offered your way, that was it, you had to buy it, so now she was a little wary. Was this the same sort of thing? Was him showing her where the supermarket was a way for him to make money?

She fished about in her bumbag and took out fifteen US dollars. He turned, perhaps to check whether she was following him. His attention on the money didn't last long. He shook his head and seemed offended that she held it out to him.

"No, put it away. Please. This is free."

He really did seem genuine, so she did as he'd asked, drawing the zip across on her bag. As they walked, Freya a few steps behind him, he launched into some facts about Jamaica.

"You see that?" He jabbed a finger in the air at some tree-covered hills. "Famous people live up there. Mick Jagger is one of them."

She had no idea if that was bullshit, but she'd be on Google later when she could use the hotel Wi-Fi.

"Where are you from?" he asked.

"London."

"Ah, I have family in Leeds. Maybe if I come to England, you can show me around."

There was no way she'd be doing that. "Leeds is a fair trek from London."

He chatted away about England and Jamaica being linked, a fact she hadn't known, then he stopped to reach up and pluck something from a tree in someone's front garden.

"This is an almond."

For some reason, she'd thought almonds grew on the tree in their shells, but what he showed her was encased in a green pod. He held it towards her, and she was reticent to take it in case he charged her for it, even though he'd stolen it. Were people allowed to just pick things from other people's gardens around here?

"Let me show you something else, but we need to cross the road first," he said.

She stared over to the left. A narrow turn-off track in front of a large, posh white house surrounded by many trees. Grass separated the track from the main road, and because of the busy traffic and his friendly demeanour, she didn't feel like she was under threat.

Cool Raffia walked out into the middle of the road and held up his hands to stop the cars, urging her to run across. She obeyed him, feeling awkward because she wanted to do the walk by herself yet at the same time didn't want to offend him. The knowledge he'd shared with her so far had been interesting, and what if he was lonely and just wanted someone to talk to? That's how he came across.

In front of the house, he pulled something off another tree and squeezed it, shooting his hand towards her face. "Moses in a basket," he informed her, elongating the 'a' of basket, then he went on to give her some information about the little white flower inside the open pod. "You know, Moses from the Bible? We call it that because it looks like a baby in a basket."

She didn't know whether that was true either so smiled and glanced along the track. Another house stood at the end, but this one didn't belong to anyone rich. Again, no windows, and despite cars, vans, and coaches speeding by, there was a desolate feel to the area, as if an invisible wall had been built between the road and the properties, abandonment and quiet on one side, busyness and noise on the other.

"We need to cross the road again." Cool Raffia ambled off, the rocking motion of his walk giving the impression that his knee possibly hurt. He repeated his

actions from earlier, holding his arms up so she could get across.

Back on the right-hand side, he trundled ahead of her, stopping to pluck a long leaf from someone else's front garden. He ripped a part of it off and pressed it into her hand. She refused to curl her fingers around it.

"Squeeze it," he said, "then smell it on your skin."

If she had to pay a few dollars for taking this piece of plant, then she would, because it was clear he wasn't going to let her walk on until she'd done what he wanted. She sniffed, and the smell reminded her of Christmas when her nan used to press dried cloves into an orange. Cool Raffia told her what the leaf was, but she didn't take the information in. To be honest, she was getting overheated now and irritable, and while she really ought to be grateful that he was taking the time to tell her these things, she just wanted to get to the sodding shop.

A car slowed to a stop right by her, the passenger window going down. Someone in the driver's seat leaned across and said, "You're in good hands with Cool Raffia," then he pointed two fingers at her in the shape of a gun and drove off.

Had she just imagined that? No, he'd definitely done it, but maybe she'd seen it as a gun when he'd literally just been pointing at her. She checked where her guide was, and he'd wandered ahead. She told herself that the man in the car must be Cool Raffia's friend or something, that maybe they belonged to the same community. She caught up with him. He talked some more about Jamaica until just past another little house, a row of shops appeared as well as a dusty petrol station forecourt. Freya walked across it, thanking him for accompanying her there, eager to get her stuff in the supermarket and go back to the hotel.

"You go into the supermarket," he said behind her. "I'll go and get my taxi so I can give you a lift back."

She was about to tell him that it was fine, she'd walk, but he'd already gone. She pushed open the supermarket door, so relieved there was air-conditioning, and looked around for a basket or trolley. Finding neither, she started at one end, intending to go down every aisle until she found the sun cream, praying it wasn't going to cost her an arm and a leg.

Chapter Two

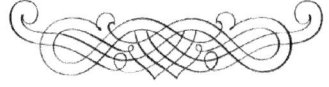

On his trips to England, Big B missed being able to smoke the good stuff wherever he went and whenever he wanted. In the flat he was borrowing, one of the next-door neighbours kept coming round and complaining about the smell. She was here again, a woman with brown hair, floppy tits, and a big arse, hands on her hips.

"If you don't stop blowing that shit through those fucking balcony doors so the stink comes round to my flat, I'm going to phone the police."

He could antagonise her, tell her to fuck off, or even threaten her in a much more impressive way than she'd just threatened him, but regardless of her bluster, he didn't think she'd phone the police. He only had enough for personal use anyway, and he could claim it was medicinal. But instead of going down the wrong road, he smiled at her and held the joint up, choosing the *high* road. For once. Something he wanted to do more often, but he'd been so used to being a shitty gang member for so long that he'd forgotten how to behave like a normal human being if he wasn't with his family. But he had to try if he wanted to turn over a new leaf.

"You might feel better if you smoke some," he said. "You should live by the mantra, 'Don't worry, be happy'."

"How can I fucking do that when I've got mouths to feed and bills to pay, eh? I've got my washing out on my balcony, and my kids are going to smell like pot when they go to school tomorrow because that smoke keeps going all over their uniforms. It isn't right, what you're doing."

"I'll stop it after I finish this one, all right?"

"You'd better."

She stomped off along the walkway to her door, giving him a glare and tutting, going inside. Maybe if he wasn't feeling so free and easy at the moment, what with the marijuana doing its work, he might worry more about the police turning up, asking him why he was here, digging deeper. He'd be right in the shit if that happened; he was supposed to stay under the radar, not jeopardise the operation.

Sometimes he wished he'd never agreed to become a part of this. The money was good, and being a big cheese in his hometown in Jamaica had its benefits, but the risk they took every time they did this…not good.

He disliked the visits to England. It confused him as to why anyone would want to live somewhere with year-round rain—or it seemed that way to him, this week so far being the exception. Then again, it rained in Jamaica, except the air was still hot, the humidity off the scale. What he didn't like was the coldness to the English rain, the dreariness, and how it seemed to turn all the colours grey. The two countries were worlds apart, but he never felt alone while he was in the UK. There were pockets of Jamaica here he could dive into—or hide in—if he chose to. The community welcomed him with a roared "Wagwan!" and a slap on the back.

He returned inside and continued smoking from his perch on the sofa, staring out through the open balcony doors that let in the balmy summer air. The evening was drawing closer, and soon he'd get a message from back home to tell him to stay put for a little while longer until someone came over to help him out, something he'd already been told three times.

This was the bit he hated. The wait. At this point, he just wanted to go home, but there was still the cargo to deal with. Now it was a case of trusting the UK contacts to do their part until it was time to move the goods on. The contacts were new to him this time, white men recommended by one of the Jamaican community, although he didn't like the fact that he had to meet them with their faces covered. Yeah, he understood it, their need for anonymity, but he hated it that they could see his face and he couldn't see theirs. He'd felt vulnerable.

He inhaled some more weed then blew the smoke out, watching it puff into the air and slowly drift towards the balcony doors. It reminded him of looking through the plane window at the clouds on his way here, and he had an extremely strong yearning to go home, to stop doing this shit.

His luck was going to run out one day, he could feel it in his bones, but if he stayed here he'd have to hide forever, and if he went home and announced he was leaving the gang, he'd have to face the barrel of a gun.

Chapter Three

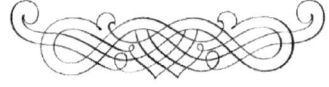

Eamon "Puggy" Puggle had been asked to work for Fish and Chips again. Chips was all right, if abrupt sometimes, but Fish could be scary, and he'd hit Puggy once. He'd promised never to do it again, said he felt guilty, but Puggy was all too aware of how people could change. How they lied. Because Fish and Chips had lied.

They'd said they didn't need him anymore now that he wasn't storing the drugs and passing them on to customers at the front door. They'd said they wouldn't come back.

But they had.

The thing was, Puggy liked the money. This new job paid just as much as before, although this time he wasn't allowed to stand at the front door talking to whoever came to pick up coke. Instead, he had to look after what he'd been told to call 'cargo'. He called it that whenever he was with Fish and Chips, but when he was on his own, he called it what it really represented.

Income.

Since Shawnee had cleaned his flat for him, Puggy had been able to keep on top of it himself. The woman from the social, Miss Daulton, was ever so pleased with him. He liked to make her happy because then it meant she didn't stay for long. If she was unhappy with his progress, she sat there for about an hour and kept asking him questions.

People weren't allowed to ask questions at the moment.

Not while Income was there.

He stood in front of the sink unit and stared out of his kitchen window in his ground-floor flat, missing the times he'd wait right in this spot for the customers to come by. He knew selling drugs was wrong, and he knew he was being used because of his medical issues and how stupid he came across sometimes, but the joke was on them because he was well aware of how people viewed him. Like his mum had told him, there would be times his condition could be used to his advantage, for him to get on better in life, and if that meant playing on it, then he should. Other times, though, he felt so lost and confused.

He, more than anyone, was well aware of how his brain didn't work like everyone else's, he even smelled things different, heard and saw them different. He liked patterns and order as much as possible, they comforted him, but he was getting better at being surprised, like when Fish and Chips had come round to talk to him about Income. For once, he hadn't been upset or shocked that they'd turned up without asking because it had been lonely on his own.

He didn't understand why sometimes he hated it and sometimes it was okay. It tired him trying to work his brain out.

Kids played on the grass, kicking a football to each other. They lived in this block and sometimes caused aggro out the front. They were rude to residents and picked on other kids, swearing a lot and laughing. Puggy didn't like watching them be bullies. He'd been through it a lot at school, people taking the piss out of him because he wasn't like them. Whenever he spotted these lads being nasty to anyone, he went out there and told them to pack it in, then they turned on him instead, but better that than the original victim continuing to cop it. Every now and again Puggy caught himself wishing he was normal, but if being normal meant being like those lads, then he didn't want anything to do with it.

It was weird because he knew what he'd done for Fish and Chips before and what he was doing for them now was wrong, illegal, and that there was no way he should be involved, but at the same time, because it benefited him and made his life easier, made him feel better, he did it anyway. He liked being able to buy Nike tracksuits and trainers. He loved not looking like the kid he used to be, in hand-me-down clothes that Mum had got from another mum up the school. The only time he'd got something new as a child was at Christmas or his birthday.

His phone bleeped.

MISS DAULTON: ARE YOU AVAILABLE FOR ME TO POP ROUND ON MY WAY HOME FROM WORK? WOULD YOU BE COMFORTABLE WITH THAT?

Puggy thought about it. One, Income was in his spare bedroom, so was it wise to have someone in authority visiting? Two, Miss Daulton always kept to the same routine and day of visiting him, so why had it changed? Had something happened? Had someone grassed him up for working for Fish and Chips and his benefits were going to be cut? He paced in front of the window, anxiety filling his whole body, his brain a million steps ahead to where he was in prison for fraud.

PUGGY: WHY DO YOU NEED TO COME ROUND?

MISS DAULTON: I HAVE SOME GOOD NEWS REGARDING THE COMMUNITY CENTRE.

Was that all? Relief powered through him.

PUGGY: OKAY. WHAT TIME?

MISS DAULTON: I'M AT THE TRAFFIC LIGHTS BY YOUR FLAT NOW. IS THAT TOO SOON? SHOULD I SIT IN MY CAR OUTSIDE FOR A LITTLE WHILE SO YOU CAN GET USED TO THE CHANGE IN YOUR DAY?

Puggy: No, I'm all right, but thank you for understanding.

Mum had told him it didn't cost anything to be nice to someone if they were showing you they cared, and he especially didn't mind being nice to Miss Daulton who'd helped him so much. And anyway, if she had good news about the community centre, then it could only mean he'd been allowed to join the chess club and the dance club and…he didn't want to go to the flower-pressing club, but she'd put his name down for it anyway. The sole aim, she'd said, was to get him out and about, making friends with other people like him. What was the other thing she'd said? That if he could interact with others on the spectrum then he might feel better about himself. Miss Daulton had a sister with autism who found her life was so much better when she hung around with other neurodivergent people because they "just got" each other.

He didn't know what that felt like because he'd never "just got" anyone and no one had "just got" him.

"Maybe," she'd said gently, "Because these clubs are run for neurodivergent people, instead of you tiring yourself out by masking, trying to be what society considers 'normal', you'd be better off being exactly who you are."

He had to agree with her there. Masking *was* tiring. So much so that sometimes, if he had to go to the doctor's or whatever, it took a couple of days afterwards for him to settle back down again.

He sighed, because as usual, there was a downside to any rainbow that appeared in his life. The good news about the community centre would be bad news for Fish and Chips. Fish had told him he wasn't allowed to leave the flat for long while Income was there, and going out three times a week of an evening would likely be banned.

Puggy wanted to cry. He really, really wanted to be able to go to the community centre, but if he did that he'd get in trouble with Fish and Chips, and they might take Income away and pay someone else to do his job. Then he'd lose all that money. He didn't like to cook, he loved pizza takeaways, and he'd had to be so careful in budgeting his benefits to accommodate his eating habits.

A tap at the front door had him looking out of the window and craning his neck to see who was out there, but whoever it was stood out of sight. What if Fish and Chips had come? What if he had to let them in and then Miss Daulton turned up and asked who they were? They always wore balaclavas, so it was going to look so weird to her. She'd think they were robbers or something and phone the police.

He squeezed his fingers together rhythmically and set his sights on the other side of his front door, craning his neck even more, to the point a nerve twinged. But at least he could see now. Thankfully it was Miss Daulton. He shuffled into the hallway and opened the door, letting her in, a new worry forming. What if Fish and Chips came while he was talking to her?

She eyed him with concern. "Are you okay, Eamon? You look troubled. I promise you, it's *good* news from the community centre. I'm sure I said that in my text so you didn't worry."

"Yeah, you did. Do you want a cup of tea?" He hoped she didn't, but at least if she said yes he'd know she planned to be here for at least twenty minutes. In the time it took for him to make her a drink, he could sort his mind out into accepting she was staying.

"No, no, I'm literally just popping in. So, you got into all the clubs—chess, dance, and pressing flowers." She smiled. "Don't look like that, pressing flowers might not be so bad, and anyway, there's something we can do with the flowers afterwards. I've been thinking about it. I could laminate them for you, and maybe one afternoon when I'm free, and only if you want me to, I could come round and we could make some bunting with the laminated flowers and then take them to your mum. You once told me she liked bunting because it reminded her of the street parties she'd been to as a little girl."

That was a nice idea. He imagined the bunting tied to the top of her gravestone and the flowers fluttering in the breeze. Mum would definitely like it, and he was so chuffed that Miss Daulton had remembered what he'd told her. It meant she cared.

He nodded, his eyes stinging. "All right."

"Okay, so here are the times and whatnot." She handed him a leaflet from the community centre.

"Thank you," he said.

A thud came from the spare room.

Miss Daulton frowned. "What was that?"

Puggy panicked inside. "The neighbours are being very noisy at the moment."

That was what Fish had told him to say if anyone came here. Fish and Chips knew that Puggy had visits from Miss Daulton and the medication lady who popped by once a week to make sure he had everything he needed and to drop off his prescriptions. In the past he'd kept forgetting to pick his tablets up, so Miss Daulton had arranged for Mrs Kapor to pop by.

Miss Daulton frowned harder. "How are you coping with that? I know noise bothers you."

He shrugged. "It's just a few knocks and bumps on the wall. I'm trying really hard not to let things upset me."

"Let me know if it gets too much. I can go round and ask them to tone it down." She smiled and opened the front door. "I'd best be off. If you want me to go with you to the clubs, just send me a text."

She was good like that. She said things so he knew he had options, that he didn't have to do things alone if he didn't want to, but for once he was looking forward to going somewhere he could be himself and not worry about what people thought of him. Okay, he'd be nervous and probably still mask to begin with, but wouldn't it be nice to chat and laugh without a care in the world?

"I think I'll be all right," he said, "but thank you for the offer."

She stepped outside just as another thud sounded in the spare room. He shut the door, slipped the chain on, and quickly went into the kitchen to watch out of the window. She got in her car and drove away, thank God.

He leaned on the sink unit and looked at the leaflet. An introduction to dance class was tonight. He hoped it wasn't any of that tango and waltz business and that he could learn body popping instead, or that robot dancing.

Another thud.

He was going to have to go and check on Income.

He placed the leaflet on the worktop and took a deep breath. He liked the money he got but not the fact that he had to go in there from time to time and collect the stinky bucket or to put food down.

He entered the spare room and stared at the built-in cupboard. There was just about enough room to swing a cat in there. Income was only small, though, and along with a bucket there was enough room to stretch a bit, especially upwards. Puggy wouldn't like to sleep in there, which was why he tied Income to the bed at night and said that if she didn't behave, she'd have to sleep in the cupboard as well as live in there.

It was so bad, what he was doing, but there was a pair of Air Jordans he wanted, and he could buy them tomorrow once Fish and Chips had been round with some of his wages.

Chapter Four

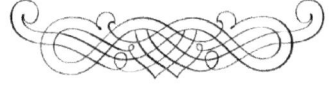

Ralph barked for George to throw the ball. The daft dog had got right into his heart ever since they'd taken him on, and he couldn't remember what life had been like without him. It certainly got George out walking in the fields behind their house, morning and evening. The problem of Ralph being alone during the week while the twins were busy had been solved by Martin who'd offered to take the dog to work with him every day. While a collie wasn't exactly bite-your-hand-off material, the type that would attack on command, something many money collectors would have preferred, as far as Martin had established, none of the customers saw Ralph as an animal who'd been brought along to add a bit of menace. After all, Martin was a calm man who didn't throw any weight around, and he'd got by all this time acting that way because he'd had something else in his arsenal to keep people in line—the fact that he worked for the twins and if he was ever harmed, then murders would happen.

George threw the ball, and Ralph galloped off after it.

George smiled at the thought of his beloved dog trotting around with Martin every weekday, getting pats and fusses off the residents, maybe even a treat or two if Martin trusted whoever had offered any.

The bloody mutt lives the life of Riley.

But that was a good thing, because George didn't have to keep him crated, except in the evenings if they were out, and by then Ralph was so tired from being with Martin that he slept. All in all, things had worked out really well on that front, and thankfully, any residents who would have recognised Ralph as previously belonging to someone else, well, they were keeping it to themselves. If rumours ever went round that they'd adopted a dog that wasn't theirs, George would stab them in the face.

While he went through the repeated motions of throwing the ball and Ralph retrieving it, he checked through the recent messages they'd received since he'd left the house half an hour ago. The reports were insignificant bullshit from their paid men on the streets, their grasses and snoops, although to be fair to them, he *had* said they should make contact no matter how small incidents were. This evening's efforts weren't anything that needed George and Greg to intervene.

A kid had been found jimmying a window of an empty, abandoned property but had run off when he'd spotted the twins' men watching. Some woman had punched her next-door neighbour over the garden fence during a row about pegs—one of them preferred to have them all matching and of the same colour, the other didn't, and an argument had erupted about which one of them was right. Some bloke had too much to drink down the Red Lion and had thrown a basket of chips at the wall when he'd been asked to calm down. And finally…

George frowned at the most recent message.

I GOT YOUR NUMBER OFF LISA AT THE ANGEL. AFTER I TOLD HER WHAT'S BEEN GOING ON, SHE SAID FOR ME TO GET HOLD OF YOU MYSELF INSTEAD OF GOING THROUGH HER BECAUSE IT WAS TOO IMPORTANT. ANYWAY, I HAVEN'T HEARD FROM MY DAUGHTER, WHICH IS CONCERNING, AND NOR HAS HER BEST FRIEND. CAN YOU HELP? HER NAME IS FREYA DUNCAN. MINE IS MARIA COLT, AND I LIVE AT 16 THE BRAMBLES.

George called out for Ralph to stop fucking about by a bush—the ball must be stuck under there—but his command went ignored. He went over there and got down on his hands and knees to find the bloody thing, then on their way back to the house, he phoned Greg who hadn't seen Maria's query in their shared WhatsApp account because he'd been busy making their dinner.

"Read the latest message," George said as soon as Greg picked up.

"Hang on."

Something sizzled in the background, probably the onions for the burgers.

"Could be nothing but it could be something," Greg said. "We're to assume that this Freya is old enough to live on her own. I see you didn't message back to get some more information out of the mother."

George took his phone from his ear and looked at WhatsApp. "I see you didn't either."

"Fuck off."

"Shall we nip round there, have a word?" George asked.

"After dinner. I didn't just slave over the stove for us to eat it later."

"I'll be back in a minute."

George ended the call, and at the edge of the field by the alley that led to their street, he threw the ball for a final time. Ralph sped off, and George waited for him at the end of the alley. He didn't bother putting the lead on for their walk to the house. George went down the side alley and entered through a door that opened into the kitchen. The smell of burgers, onions, and bacon reminded him of the food van outside Screwfix down Stanton Road. They had a sneaky snack there from time to time if they were ever out that way, which they would be this evening because The Brambles was nearby.

Greg had dished up. A towering burger sat on each plate surrounded by thick-cut chips that had been fried in a basket inside a saucepan just like their mum used to make. A wallop up of nostalgia hit George in the chest, and he cleared his throat and blinked several times to get rid of his stinging eyes.

Ralph lapped at water from his bowl and then plopped himself down on his bed inside his crate with a tired huff, his paw over his favourite pink teddy.

George hung the lead up, threw the ball in the toy basket, then washed his hands. Greg had been loading the dishwasher and now sat with George at the island.

"No talking about work until you've tasted my creation," Greg said.

George bit into the burger, chewed, and shuddered when he swallowed. "That's rank."

Greg frowned and bit into his own, then punched George on the arm. "You fucking bastard, I thought you were being serious then."

"It's bloody lush, but I didn't want to swell your head straight off the bat."

"Prick."

They ate in silence, George's mind ticking over what Maria had told them. Sons and daughters didn't contact their parents every day like they used to, but the way he looked at it, and because of their line of work, to him it made complete sense for children of *any* age to check in with their parents regularly. Fucking hell, the world was a dangerous minefield. If their mother were alive they'd be round there every day as well as texting and phoning, just to put her mind at rest.

Once he'd cleared his plate, he got up and put it in the dishwasher and rinsed his hands again as he'd got burger grease on his fingers. "Maybe Freya's got a bloke and is otherwise occupied."

"I thought the same thing," Greg said, "but it's obvious to me that the mother's used to the daughter checking in, and because she hasn't, it's rung alarm bells."

George took the phone out and added Maria to the contacts list.

GG: We'll be there in fifteen minutes. If possible, get her friend round to yours so we can speak to you both at the same time.

Maria: Thank you so much. We've been so worried.

George switched WhatsApp chats.

GG: Can any of you run a check on a Freya Duncan for me. The only address I have in relation to her is 16 The Brambles, where her mum lives.

He waited for either of their two coppers or the private detective to respond.

Anaisha: I'll do it.

George passed the latest on to Greg who was putting fresh water down in Ralph's crate. A bleep interrupted their conversation, and George stopped to read the message.

Anaisha: 23 Scotland Avenue—block of flats. Age 25. No criminal record.

GG: Cheers.

Once again, he switched chats.

GG: Go to 23 Scotland Avenue. Flats. Woman called Freya Duncan lives there and hasn't been heard from. See if she's in. If not, break in and have a look around. Report back to us as soon as possible.

Moody: Will do.

Satisfied that their man would drop everything and do as he'd been asked, George patted Ralph on the head, secured him in his crate, and opened the side door that led to the garage. "BMW, the van, or the taxi?"

Greg thought about that for a second. "I suppose it depends on whether Maria would want anyone in her street to know there's a problem. If we turn up in the BMW and these suits, then her neighbours are going to know either something's happened or think that she's in the shit with us."

"As she's messaged us, *The Brothers*, then surely she'd expect us to turn up as we are. Not everyone knows we wear disguises, and for bloody good reason."

Greg got in the BMW as his answer. On the way to The Brambles, George was tempted to ask Maria for a bit more information via message, he didn't like the way his mind was filling in the blanks, but they were nearly there so he didn't bother. Greg pulled into the cul-de-sac containing eight houses that appeared to be the four-or-more-bedroom variety, what with the size of them, and parked outside number sixteen.

George assessed the property. Clean and shiny windows, wooden Venetian blinds behind the glass. A tidy front garden, a square of grass edged with beds containing whatever red, yellow, and pink flowers currently bobbed their heads in the breeze. Gravel path, and at the end a step that led to the front door, on top of which sat two pots with miniature fir trees inside them. On the block-paved driveway, a silver Vauxhall Corsa. This visit was a far cry from any of those they'd have made regarding the messages that had come in earlier on. Thank God they wouldn't be speaking to people who'd argued about pegs.

They got out of the car, and the front door opened before they got anywhere near it. Two women stood in the frame, one slightly behind the other. The one at the front was shorter and older, with wispy, mid-length brown hair, her pale-pink gym outfit and white trainers revealing she was either home from a workout or had been about to leave when George had responded to her query. The younger woman, long blonde hair to her shoulders and light-blue eyes (that were so light they were creepy if George were honest), had flushed cheeks and looked like she'd been crying. She had a bohemian air about her in a long flowing patchwork dress and a brown Stetson knockoff perched above her pointy-chinned face.

"So sorry to trouble you like this," Maria said, "but the more me and Lottie were talking, the more we thought something had happened."

She turned and waited for Lottie to do the same, the pair of them walking off down the hallway, leaving George and Greg to follow. In a large and airy kitchen where everything had a blinding-white quality to it, George reckoned he'd leave here with a migraine. Evening sunlight streamed in through a wall of bifold doors and bounced off a blingy chandelier in the dining area that splashed sparkles of light all over the bare walls.

"That can cause a fire, you know." George nodded to some teardrops of light on a wooden bookcase painted white. "If it gets hot enough and concentrated enough. It happened once to our mum. She had a glass paperweight, and sunlight burnt a little mark on her chest of drawers. She caught it smoking."

"Goodness…"

"Anyway, how can we help?"

"Would you like a cuppa or anything?" Maria asked.

"Not for me, thanks," George said.

Greg shook his head.

Maria gestured to the dining table. "If you'd like to sit down…"

They all got settled, Maria linking her fingers and laying her hands on her lap, Lottie folding her arms so her hands hid under her armpits.

"Why did you get hold of us and not the police?" George asked.

"I did phone them, but because of the last message Freya sent, they didn't say it in so many words but it was obvious they thought I was being neurotic and worrying for no reason."

"What did her last message say?"

"To back off because I was getting on her nerves."

"What's wrong with that?" George asked.

"She wouldn't talk to me like that. She'd put it a different way."

"Like what?"

"For me to give her some space. She'd never have said I was getting on her nerves, even though I did keep messaging her. She was having an evening by herself, and it bothered me for some reason that she'd outright said she needed to be alone, so I wanted to make sure she was okay."

"But she basically said you were getting on her tits."

"Well, yes, but that wasn't until hours after I'd sent the last message, so that was weird in itself. She could have fallen asleep, I suppose, then woken up during the night to reply…"

George raised his eyebrows at Lottie. "What's your take on that?"

"I agree with Maria. Even if she *was* getting on Freya's nerves, she would never have said it."

"Do you have the kind of friendship where she would've told you if her mum was pissing her off?"

"Yes, but like we said, she'd never have said so to Maria. She'd rather say it any other way than that."

"But what if she was really naffed off at the time of sending the message?" Greg asked. "You know, when you get so boiling angry that you don't think before you speak."

Lottie shook her head. "She wasn't the type, although…"

George narrowed his eyes at her. "Although what?"

"Since she came back from Jamaica, she's been slightly different."

"In what way?"

"A bit jumpy, sharper when she speaks sometimes."

"Yet you just said she isn't the type…"

"I know, but what I mean is in general, before Jamaica, she'd never have been snippy."

"Did something happen while she was away?" George asked.

"Not that she told me," Lottie said.

"Me neither." Maria sighed. "She went on holiday to get over the split with her ex. That was unusual in itself, her going alone, but she insisted she had to learn to be by herself at some point, that me and Lottie couldn't hold her hand forever. I think that was maybe her trying desperately to prove to herself that she could do it. James had a habit of…well, he kind of took over everything so she didn't have to be put out. I don't think it was any form of coercive control, he just loved her so much that he wanted to do everything for her. She didn't let him at first, but as the relationship progressed I saw she was allowing it more and more until in the end she didn't have to lift a finger at all if she didn't want to."

"Did she keep in contact with you while she was away?"

"Every day," Maria said.

Lottie confirmed it.

"So she went away to sort her head out after a breakup, came back snippy sometimes, then said you were getting on her nerves and to leave her alone. That about the gist of it?"

Maria nodded.

"Why did she split up with James?"

"He was having an emotional affair," Lottie said. "With someone he worked with."

"So much for him loving her," Greg muttered.

"So," George said, "the poor cow found out her partner was fucking about with someone else, she went on holiday to try to get over it, possibly realised she couldn't, and when she got home everything was just as shit as it had been before she'd left, so she's hacked off and just wants to be left alone."

Maria closed her eyes for a second or two and then opened them to stare straight at George. "Ordinarily, I'd agree with you. Even Freya, gentle as she is, could lose her temper if pushed hard enough, and I really don't blame her for being snippy, she had a lot to contend with emotionally, and James was moving out of her place while she was away so she'd have had that on her mind, too, and to come back and find him not there, even though she didn't *want* him there anymore, it must have got on top of her, but... All I need you to do is to get her to open the door and find out if she's okay. If she wants to hide out until she gets her head screwed on straight, then far be it for me to interfere, but her last message to me really isn't the way she'd speak to me, no matter how she was feeling, and something in my gut is telling me there's a problem."

"I've already sent one of our men round to her place. Don't you have a key, then, to go and have a look yourself?"

"No. I *have* been round there, but all I could do was look through the letterbox and shout to ask if she was all right."

"What about where she works, have you contacted them?"

"She doesn't work weekends or Mondays, so she wouldn't be due there until tomorrow anyway, and she has the option of working from home, so she could have been doing that."

"We'll have a chat with a few people and get back to you. Is there anywhere she hangs around regularly, a pub or whatever?"

"We usually meet in the Noodle," Lottie said, "but I've been in and asked, and no one's seen her since we were last there."

"Maybe we'll get further than you when we ask questions." George smiled. "What's James's surname?"

"Shinton," Maria said. "I have no clue where he moved to, but his parents live in Partridge Close, number thirty-eight."

George's phone beeped.

MOODY: HERE. GOING IN NOW.

George turned the screen round to show Maria and Lottie. "We'll sit tight until another message comes through, so if an offer of a cuppa is still on the table, I'll have a coffee, thanks."

Chapter Five

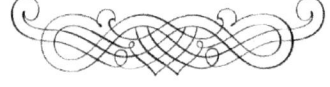

The sun cream had cost eight US dollars. Freya had bought two, plus a bottle of water for forty cents and a packet of gummy bears for eighty. She paid for her things, alarmed that at the door she had to open her bag and show the contents and the receipt to the surly female security guard. Was that because she wasn't a local? Didn't they trust strangers around here?

RAFFIA

So far, Freya had discovered the people she'd encountered on this holiday were either moody, rude and abrupt, or extra happy, smiley, and kind. None one seemed to be in between. A few had even rolled their eyes at her as though she was stupid, all for just asking for coffee at breakfast or an orange juice with lunch, and she'd been tempted to complain to the rep. While she understood that everybody got in a bad mood sometimes, her days were a minefield when she dealt with the hotel staff because she didn't know what reception she was going to get. Still, she'd made the decision to come here, even though some of the reviews had stated that certain staff members needed lessons in manners.

She pushed open the supermarket door and stepped outside, the heat immediately smacking into her face, the wet humidity clutching at the skin on her exposed arms and legs. She'd spent most of this holiday feeling wet with sweat unless she was in the air-conditioned sports bar or her room. No wonder so many people kept dipping in and out of the swimming pools and the sea.

She checked her surroundings, specifically looking for a taxi and Cool Raffia sitting in the driver's seat — so she could avoid him. She really didn't want to see him or to have to deal with him again, or to be firmer and mean it when she said no. She always felt icky if she had to be overly harsh with someone.

A couple of cars were parked at the pumps, their owners filling up with petrol and having a conversation about someone called Hot Cherry. A woman walked into the pharmacy with a baby strapped to her chest. Traffic sped up and down the main road, no Cool Raffia in sight, so Freya settled the handles of the carrier bag in the crook of her elbow, took out the bottle of water, and headed past the petrol station building.

On the grass verge, she gulped down some water and put the bottle back in the bag. She'd made it a few yards when the sound of someone's feet shuffling the dry grass behind caught her attention. Oh God, was Cool Raffia following her, or was it someone else? She peered over her shoulder, spotting the now familiar gait of the man who'd walked with her to the shops. She faced ahead again and upped her pace, annoyed that she felt vulnerable now, despite there being people in cars whizzing past.

"Wait!" Cool Raffia shouted. "I've got my taxi."

She didn't want to wait, she didn't want to get in the taxi, and if he'd collected it, why was he following her on foot?

She called back, "I'm walking."

She pressed on, faster, unease twisting her gut, which was probably because she didn't like confrontation, and if Cool Raffia kept pushing for her to get in his taxi, something she most certainly didn't want to do, then she was going to have to say something to him.

She caught sight of him in the corner of her eye. Honestly, she hadn't expected him to be able to move that fast with his dodgy leg, but he was gaining on her quickly. Her stomach rolled over when she checked over her shoulder again. A white people-carrier type van with blacked-out windows drew up behind him. It parked on the verge. What the fucking hell was going on here?

Despite the heat, a sluice of cold sweat covered Freya, and she turned to face ahead and walked even faster. Traffic continued to scoot by. The grass continued to shuffle. Then Cool Raffia was beside her, kind of sideways skipping with his back to the road, one hand in his shorts pocket. She was aware that the white van was still there and imagined how many people were inside. Only the driver and front passenger, or were the other seats filled as well? Should she try to make it to the hotel or take a chance and sprint past the van and return to the safety of the supermarket? Call for an Uber there?

"Do you want to buy some of the good stuff, the Bob Marley?" Cool Raffia asked her.

She carried on walking, her heart thumping hard. "No thank you."

He held out a small package. She ignored it, so he put it in his pocket.

"Then you need to pay me for the tour."

So that was what he was calling it, was it, a tour? Yet earlier he'd just wanted to point her to the shops for free, *she distinctly remembered him saying that word. What a fucking liar. Angry that someone had successfully tricked her, making her think he was a nice person, she had to stop herself from telling him to fuck off. When she'd dumped her ex, she'd vowed never to be taken in by a man again, yet here she was…*

Still making for the safety of the hotel, she glanced across at Cool Raffia. His face had completely changed from a happy-go-lucky local to a spiteful and scary drug dealer. He put a clammy hand on her arm to stop her, and the man in the car from earlier flew along and tooted his horn. Was that a signal she was still in safe hands with Cool Raffia?

I don't think so.

She opened her bumbag and took out the fifteen dollars she'd offered him earlier.

"More," he said, eyes narrowed.

Shit, she'd let him see how much of a wedge she had, but it was mainly one-dollar bills so it seemed like she had more than she did. She moved her hand to count out another five inside the bag, bringing it out.

"More."

"That's enough now," she said, although maybe she shouldn't have because a dark cloud had taken over his expression.

"I said more. You've got it. Forty dollars."

His tone meant she obeyed. She counted the notes one by one, grateful he wasn't asking for her phone or bank cards. But was that going to come next? She was so conscious of that van still being parked on the verge, and it dawned on her then that this must be one of those scams you read about online. Had the man in the car who'd told her she was safe been something to do with this? Since it was obvious she'd refused a taxi ride, which she'd likely have been charged an extortionate rate for, had the van come along because it contained people who'd harm her if she didn't buy drugs or pay for the tour? She had no choice but to give him the money—fucking hell, she'd give him all of it if it meant he'd leave her alone.

She handed him the cash, and he snatched it from her then loped off towards the van. She shot off, almost running, then peeked over her shoulder. Cool Raffia got in the van, and it drove past her. A hand emerged from the partially open passenger window, shaped like a gun. What was *that, some kind of gang sign, because that other driver had done the same. Had they sent out a man who looked like he wouldn't hurt a fly, making her feel comfortable in his company, just a lonely bloke wanting to help, when really he belonged to a scamming outfit?*

As the van disappeared in the distance, she thought of all the scenarios that could have happened. She'd got away lightly, only having to hand over forty dollars. Maybe he hadn't pushed her for more or asked for her belongings because he'd seen which hotel she was staying at. He must know she'd had to sign out of the resort and if she didn't sign back in then the police might become involved.

With her mind ticking over and over what had happened and how she'd been drawn in, how she'd trusted him, she ignored the beeping horns and powered onwards. With the hotel boundary hedge in sight, she sighed in relief and almost cried at how happy she was to have got this far. Then a herd of goats suddenly appeared from the front garden of the little windowless house beside the hotel, and it felt like she was in some kind of weird universe. She'd just been a victim of the tricks she'd read about in the paper, and now a load of animals were galloping towards her.

Once she was close to the hedge, she poked her head around it to see if Cool Raffia stood against the lamppost. No one was there, so she went to the guards' table and signed the book.

"There was a man in a yellow football shirt out there when I left," she said, "and he just forced me to pay him forty dollars."

The woman guard sucked her teeth. "Talk to him about it."

Freya turned to the young man and told him everything that had happened. Surely they'd want to know about this sort of thing. Local scammers were hardly a good advertisement for the hotel.

The man laughed. "You got lucky. If I'd given you the tour, I'd have charged you sixty."

She stared at him in shock. He thought this was funny*? What the fuck was funny about basically being robbed in broad daylight? What the fuck was funny about convincing a woman on her own to trust you, then you switched personalities later on because she didn't do what you wanted? She was actually speechless, had no clue what to say in response, so she marched off down the driveway.*

The taxi driver from earlier ran across the road and came up to her again.

By this point she'd had enough, and because she felt safe on the resort grounds, she snapped, "I don't want a bloody taxi, okay?"

"I just wanted to tell you that I misquoted you earlier."

She already knew he had. He'd said two-fifty then three-fifty. She stared at him.

"I went into the office to check, and the proper price to Negril is three hundred."

"Right." She smiled to be polite and walked on.

"Will you take my card?" He followed her and held one out.

She took it, stuffed it in her bumbag, and hurried closer to the hotel. By the splash park, she relaxed upon hearing voices and laughter and the gushing water. A little farther on was an area where staff smoked cigarettes beside wheelie bins—or, going by the now familiar smell, weed.

One of them gave her a big smile and shouted out, "Wagwan!"

She smiled back—she didn't have it in her to return the greeting—and put on a spurt of speed. A few metres from the hotel steps, she sagged, her irritation spiking. Along with a couple of coaches dropping off or picking up holidaymakers were two battered taxis, their drivers leaning against their vehicles. One of them held out a card to her, the name Benny Bean scrawled along the top in blue pen. She'd read about him in the reviews, someone not to be trusted apparently, so she shook her head to decline the card and rushed up the steps.

She headed straight for the rep behind the desk.

"Did you get everything you needed at the supermarket?" the rep asked.

Sour from her experience, hot and bothered and fucking annoyed, Freya said, "I may as well have just paid the high prices in that boutique for the sun cream because I ended up handing over a fortune anyway."

The rep frowned. "What do you mean?"

Freya told her what had gone on, getting angrier and angrier as she went, mainly at herself for being so bloody naïve. She should have known exactly who Cool Raffia really was.

The rep's eyebrows shot up. "That's never happened before."

What a load of bollocks.

"That you know of," Freya said. "Maybe people don't feel like they can complain about something like that because they're too scared to."

"I'm very sorry that happened to you."

"Are you?" Freya stormed off across the foyer to stand on the balcony that ran the width of the hotel and faced the beach.

She stared out at the water and took in a few deep breaths, keeping in time with the gentle waves, and told herself she was safe—or as safe as she could keep herself until she left this place. No more walking to the farthest end of the beach for her. Definitely no more walks to the supermarket. She'd keep away from the shrubbery in the hotel grounds, and there was no way she'd be taking any "Bob Marley" from those men who sat on the opposite end of the beach by the scuba diving building. She doubted very much they were employed by the hotel, and who knew, they might be part of Cool Raffia's gang. God, her mind was going in all different directions now.

At least he'd only asked for forty dollars.

At least she wasn't dead.

She made her way to the lift and went back to her room, the blast of cold air-conditioning beautiful on her skin. The housekeeping lady had been in. A swan made of dusky-pink towels sat on the bed, pretty red flowers and some rose petals scattered on the white sheets. She put those in the bin and shook the swan out, folding the towel and placing it in the bathroom. Then she realised she hadn't taken a picture. Each day she'd sent a photo of the towel animals to Lottie.

She had the sudden need to tell her about what had happened, but Lottie was the panicking type, and she'd suggest Freya got on the next plane home and demanded compensation from the tour operator. Unable to deal with that, Freya had a shower instead, washing away Cool Raffia's touch on her arm. It was just a shame she couldn't erase the image of his face from her brain. That expression when he'd switched from the nice man into the nasty...she didn't think she'd ever forget it.

Then the taxi driver's words popped into her head: "You should let me take you..." Had he said that because he'd known there'd be a scammer waiting for her and he'd wanted to keep her safe? Should she have listened to him and got in his taxi? Yes, she bloody should, but it was too late, she'd been through the experience and now had to live with the memory of it.

Chapter Six

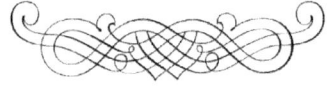

Gloves on, Moody had used a lock pick to get into Freya's flat and, with the door closed quietly behind him, he stood in the narrow hallway listening for any sounds within and without. From what he'd gathered on his way up here using the communal stairs, each of the three floors had four flats. The last thing he needed was a neighbour to come nosing and find he'd broken in, but then again, a neighbour may very well be his next port of call if the twins told him he had to nip around there.

It concerned him that a young woman hadn't been heard from for a few days, and it especially concerned him that this flat was *so* still and quiet. The type of quiet that spoke of dead people in the next room. He'd tapped on the front door and called through the letterbox already, which would have alerted the neighbours if they'd heard him, yet no one had come out. Did that mean Freya didn't have that kind of relationship with those she lived by? Did they all keep to themselves? If she was here, perhaps she'd heard him and decided to hide for whatever reason.

Or was that him just being fanciful?

He smiled at the recollection of being ill as a kid, his mother having to go to work, leaving him on his own, her words ringing in his ears that he mustn't open the door to anyone—"*Anyone*, do you hear me?" He used to hide in the cupboard under the stairs if someone rang the bell or knocked, but surely a grown woman wouldn't do that, not unless she was afraid of someone. If she was, then he could imagine her hiding in a wardrobe or something, in the hope that whoever had come to call wouldn't find her.

But maybe this was just a case of someone wanting to hide in a different way—hiding from the world and all the shitty things in it. Moody sometimes got overwhelmed, so he took himself off in his van and parked in a lay-by in the countryside to get a bit of order in his head. Peace. She could be holed up in a Premier Inn, but then again, he supposed the twins would have asked their copper to look into that already.

He messaged them about it.

GG: Good shout. We'll get someone on it.

Moody had switched his phone sounds off before he'd entered the block and was glad for it now as it vibrated in his pocket. He cocked an ear to further listen for any movement in the flat, but it had that honest-to-goodness empty feel to it that he knew no one was there. He quickly took his phone out and read the message.

GG: Just so you've got a bit more info. Her ex is called James. He moved out recently after they split. We'll be going to see him once you've finished. If she's not around, let us know, then question neighbours.

Moody: Will do.

He slipped his phone back in his pocket and methodically searched the flat. On his second go round, he took more time to study his surroundings. She was neat and tidy, not a thing was out of place apart from a smashed vase on the floor in the living room. It didn't necessarily ring alarm bells. A window was open slightly, and a voile curtain moved in the breeze. It could have knocked the vase off the sill, and seeing as there was an empty space where it might have stood between two photo frames, he wasn't unduly concerned. Still, it could very well have been knocked off in a struggle, although nothing else in the vicinity indicated that was the case.

He peered at the photos. Both had the same woman in them, and she stood with a man in one and a woman in the other. The man was possibly James or a brother, and the woman a friend as they looked around the same age. If the photo of the ex was here, did that mean she still cared for him regardless of him being an ex? Maybe she wasn't the sort of bunny boiler to rip it out of the frame and slash it to pieces with a knife. Some women did allow their former partners to leave with all their clothes intact and their cars not burning.

He took a photo of the two friends just in case he needed it later.

He moved back into the bedroom. The bed had been made, a brown teddy bear sitting between the two sets of pillows. It had a love heart on its belly, and he wondered whether James had bought it for her and she couldn't stand to part with it. The drawers on one side held various women's clothes and items, but those on the other side were empty. A suitcase lay under the bed, and he pulled it out to read the loop of paper sticker going through the handle with barcodes on it, a flight number, Freya's name, and the date which showed she'd recently been on holiday.

Moody took several pictures of the sticker to show each individual part of it and put them in the WhatsApp group, adding the caption: WHERE DID SHE GO?

He opened the case to find it empty.

GG: JAMAICA. GOT ANYTHING ELSE WE NEED TO KNOW?

Moody returned to the living room and took a picture of the broken vase and the windowsill it may have fallen from. He passed on his suspicions about the curtain in the breeze.

RAFFIA

GG: Her mum asked if you can shut the window and find the spare set of keys in the top drawer of the sideboard behind the sofa. There's a fluffy key ring on it.

Moody went over there and found them straight away, then gave the rest of the drawers a quick nose through, plus the cupboards either side. He checked the kitchen cupboards, then the one in the bathroom that held the boiler and the water tank. Next he returned to the spare bedroom. Three clothes airers held a lot of washing that was now dry, mainly summer dresses and the like, so he assumed this was all of her laundry from when she'd been on holiday.

Moody: All is clear here other than the vase. Got the keys. I'll just check the bins, then I'll speak to the neighbours.

There was nothing in the bathroom bin, the same with the kitchen.

Moody: Can you ask the mother if her daughter is usually so tidy. There's fuck all in the bins.

GG: Yep, that's all normal.

Moody shut the living room window but left the vase where it was. At some point the police may need to come in here. He'd rather leave everything as he'd found it, but when the twins ordered him to do something, he did it, and he supposed closing a window was sensible. If it tipped it down, the rain could get in.

He needed some guidance on what he was and wasn't allowed to say to the neighbours, so he sent a message asking for clarification. His phone rang, and he answered it, relieved there wouldn't be the faff of sending messages backwards and forwards when all he wanted to do was get on with his job as quickly as possible then go home. He hadn't seen his missus for hours, and he missed her.

"We don't really want to alert anyone to the fact that something's wrong," George said, "although that's going to be difficult, considering you'll be asking questions as to when Freya was last seen. It's going to look well fucking dodgy because her ex has not long moved out, and you know what some people are like, they put two and two together and come up with fifty. The next thing we know, there'll be rumours going round that James has killed Freya. That sort of chat isn't needed, especially if something dodgy has gone on. If something bad has happened to her, we don't want whoever did it to know we're on their tail."

Unfortunately, with the amount of armchair detectives that had sprouted up in recent years on social media, they didn't just keep their musings to the internet. Back in the day it had been called plain old gossiping, and instead of a virtual wall, the chat played out in streets and supermarkets and the school playground at pickup time. It likely still did, *then* everyone plastered it on their wall.

"So how do you want me to play this?" he asked. "Whatever way we spin it, I'm still asking the same question: have you seen your neighbour?"

"True. Okay, fuck it, make out you're a copper. So you come off as authentic, her mum's name's Maria and her best friend is called Lottie. Neither of them have heard from her for three days, so we're talking Friday as the last possible sighting of her at her flat. At the moment it would probably look like she's gone away for a long weekend. Tell them it's a welfare check, nothing sinister."

"I'll do it now."

Moody cut the call, put the phone in his pocket and, Freya's keys in hand, he left the flat and knocked on the one next door. A scruffy bare-chested bloke with a long blond perm opened up and stared at him through narrowed eyes and a fog of smoke coming from a joint held between two tobacco-stained fingers.

"Yeah?" He sniffed then took a drag of his weed.

Moody didn't hold out much hope in finding answers, but he'd give it a go anyway. "Do you know the woman next door?"

"Freya? Yeah, sort of, why?"

"I'm Detective Sergeant Forbes—and there's no need to look alarmed, I don't give a shit about your joint. I've been asked to do a welfare check by Freya's mother who hasn't heard from her for a few days. Since Friday, actually."

"Let me just get rid of this. There's something fucking weird about smoking this shit in front of a copper." The man left the door open and disappeared into another room. He came back and folded his arms, leaning against the jamb. "Friday. Yeah, I saw her after work, so that would have been about quarter past six. I remember the time because I was naffed off I was three-quarters of an hour late leaving a job. I'm a plumber, and some fanny at the school round the corner thought it'd be funny to take a hammer into the bogs and smack a hole in one of the pipes. Me and my boss went there thinking it would be a simple case of switching pipes out, but it turned into a three-hour stint."

"So, you saw her?" Moody prompted.

"Yeah, she was coming out of her flat as I was going in mine. She stared at the state of me because my clothes were wet, and I explained what had gone on up at the school then said it was a story James would find funny—I have no idea if he would, like, it was just my way of finding out where he'd gone. About three weeks ago she went off with a suitcase, then he moved out. I was just being a nosy bastard for my missus because she'd wanted to know what was going on but hadn't had the balls to ask. Freya said that if I wanted to tell James the story then I'd have to go and find him because they'd split up and she didn't know where he was. I felt awkward and said I'd better go in and have a shower, and she said she was off up the shop to get a bottle of wine and a pizza from the takeaway."

Sometimes Moody hit the jackpot, and today was one of those days where he hadn't expected much but the neighbour had come up trumps. Shops had CCTV, and hopefully he'd be able to persuade the owners to show it to him—providing they still had the feed from Friday. It would be shitty fucking luck if they didn't.

"Did you hear her come back from the shop?" Moody asked.

"Nah, me and the missus decided to go out for a few bevvies up the Noodle, didn't we. I had the quickest shower on record, then we fucked off out."

"What time was that?"

"Had to be about half six. It takes five minutes to walk there, but we stopped on the way to chat to a mate of mine—his name's Tazzy Pelm if you need to know, lives down Orange Walk, number three—so we must have got to the Noodle about ten to seven, something like that."

Moody was used to people giving him information once he'd mentioned he worked for the twins, but this bloke was being extra helpful, probably because he thought Moody was DS Forbes.

I'll have to use this name more often.

"Thank you very much for your help."

"Did you want to speak to my missus to back up what I said? Because she was here when I got home Friday. She was earwigging behind the door when she saw me talking to Freya. You know, because she wanted to know what happened with James and whatnot."

"No, that's absolutely fine. Did you happen to hear anything falling and breaking next door over the weekend?" Moody flipped the keys round his finger on purpose so the man could see them. "Freya's mother gave us the keys so we could go and check the flat, and I found something in there that might be of concern."

"What's that then?"

"A vase was broken on the floor."

"Ah, now you come to mention it, I heard something in the early hours of Saturday morning. It woke me up, and I went back to sleep thinking I'd imagined it."

"Thank you very much for your time, Mr...?"

"Kevin Marsh."

Moody filed that in his memory, said goodbye, and moved along to the next neighbour. Kevin had closed his door, but Moody could imagine, if Kevin's girlfriend had been listening in on their conversation, that the pair of them were listening now. The other two neighbours on this floor hadn't seen or heard Freya since before she'd gone to Jamaica, although they both mentioned seeing James move out.

"We're not the type to make friends with neighbours, though," the woman at the end of the row said, "not after the last place we lived where everyone knew everyone's business. It was a bloody nightmare. Anyway, there's not much else I can tell you other than they were a quiet couple."

Moody left that level and went down one, quickly checking in with all those residents. Only the neighbour living below Freya had heard something thud and smash in the early hours of Saturday morning, but because there were no raised voices she'd assumed it wasn't due to an argument so hadn't thought anything else of it.

He spoke to the remaining neighbours on other levels. No one had anything to report. In the car, he phoned George and told him everything he'd found out. "It sounds like a lot of fuck all, but at least there's the shop she went to on Friday, and the takeaway. Do you want me to go there?"

"Please," George said. "Now we've been given James's new address, we'll definitely be paying him a visit. Don't pretend to be a copper when you're at the shops. If you're after CCTV, I doubt very much you'd get it unless you had an ID card. Best to just say you work for us. Keep in touch."

"Goes without saying."

Moody popped his phone away and drove off, turning left until he reached a small parade of shops. The car park in front wasn't too busy, so he managed to find a spot close to the Tesco Express. There was also a newsagent's, so she could have bought the wine in either of those. He chose Tesco first, meeting resistance from the lad behind the counter until Moody mentioned that he worked for The Brothers. Miraculously, the lad recognised Freya from the picture Moody had taken in the flat, saying he was at work all of Friday evening and she hadn't come in.

In the newsagent's two shops down, the owner, Mr Balakrishnan, gave Moody a big smile when he announced he was there on behalf of the twins. Moody explained his reason for calling in.

"Freya came in on the Friday, yes," Mr Balakrishnan said. "She talked to me, telling me about her holiday to Jamaica."

"How did she seem to you?"

"She said she had an unhappy experience while she was there but didn't say what it was, and I didn't want to press her. Whatever it was, it seemed to make her angry. She also said she had broken up with James, which was a shame, because they always popped in here every Friday and Saturday to get supplies for their television marathons." Mr Balakrishnan smiled. "But it just goes to show that what people expose to you on the outside isn't necessarily what's going on behind closed doors."

Does he know more than he's letting on?

"What do you mean by that?" Moody asked.

"Just that I would have sworn they were the perfect couple, when they can't have been if they split up."

"I see. Do you remember what she bought on Friday?"

"A bottle of prosecco and a packet of Haribo, saying that they'd been an extortionate price abroad—they'd cost ten US dollars there, and that's why my conversation with Freya has stuck in my mind so much. That's a lot of money for a few sweets. She left here at half past six, and I know that for a fact because my phone alarm went off for me to take my tablets, so she said she'd better get on and leave me to it. I asked her what she was doing for the evening, and she said she was off to get a pizza next door, then she was going home to spend the night on the sofa on her own."

"Thank you very much for your help, the twins will be pleased."

Mr Balakrishnan nodded. "I'm glad to help. Do you think Freya is missing?"

"Why would you ask that?"

"Because like I said, she and James used to come in here every Friday and Saturday, and apart from when she went to Jamaica... She wasn't in on Saturday, that's what I'm trying to say."

"Friday was the last time she got in contact with her mother."

"Oh God, I hope nothing has happened to her."

"That's what we intend to find out. Can I have a quick look at your CCTV?"

Mr Balakrishnan beckoned him around the counter, showing him how to work the equipment so he could get on with serving some customers who'd just come in. Moody selected the correct time frame and sat on a little foldout camping chair to watch the footage on a little TV under the counter. Freya entered the shop. He also viewed her exit, and she walked along towards the pizza place, going out of sight.

Moody waited for the customers to leave, then said, "If you can keep your ears and eyes open but your mouth shut…"

"I understand. Creating mass panic about someone going missing may be detrimental to what you're trying to achieve. I watch the television…"

Moody said goodbye and nipped into the pizza shop. The place was open-plan, so you could watch the pizzas being prepared. Three people worked on food, and another stood behind the counter, a spotty kid with a name tag that said Jordy.

Moody showed him Freya's picture. "Were you working here on Friday evening?"

Jordy looked at the image. "Yep."

"I'm asking on behalf of The Brothers, and they want to know whether she came in here."

"She always does, although she usually has a bloke with her, but there were a couple of weekends she didn't come in recently, although she was really brown when she was in here Friday, so I assume she'd been on holiday."

"Do you remember what she ordered?"

"A margarita with onion. He used to have pepperoni."

Moody wasn't sure whether to be impressed or creeped out by the lad's memory regarding who had what pizza. "Is it possible to look at your CCTV?"

Jordy turned and spoke to one of the people throwing pizza dough around in the air, mentioning that Moody was there for the twins. He received a nod and gestured for Moody to follow him through into an office. Once again, he viewed Freya entering and then leaving the shop, but after that, nothing.

"What's that there?" Jordy pointed to the car park.

Two men leaned on the side of a car, a dark-coloured Jaguar S Type, their faces turned away from the shops. They watched Freya after she'd gone past them. Moody did a quick calculation in his head to work out if she was going in the direction of her flat. She was. He fast-forwarded the footage along five minutes. The men got in their car and drove away in the same direction

Freya had gone. That might not be suspicious. They could have just been admiring a woman, had a chat for a while, and then drove home. The direction could have been a coincidence, but just in case, Moody asked for a copy of the footage.

With possibly the last sighting of Freya in his pocket on a flash drive, he got in his car and phoned George, passing on everything he'd learned.

"Go round to Colin's and give him the footage," George said. "Fucking good work tonight, mate."

"Thanks. Have you spoken to James?"

"Not yet. We're just leaving Freya's mother's house now. We were waiting on the outcome of your little jaunt before we did anything ourselves. Go home and get some rest because you might be needed in the next couple of hours, depending on what we discover."

Moody phoned home and asked if his missus fancied a pizza. She'd been working a late shift today, and he'd caught her just in time before she'd put something in the oven. He returned to the takeaway and ordered a fifteen-inch Meat Feast Beast, his mouth watering but his mind on a woman who seemed to have vanished into thin air.

That just wasn't possible, so were those men in the Jag responsible?

Chapter Seven

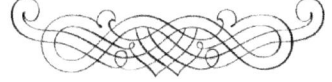

Puggy walked into the community centre, unsure where he needed to go. The front door opened into an empty foyer, toilets to the right, a doorway to his left, and ahead a massive corkboard on the wall with lots of leaflets pinned to it. He wasn't sure if the white poster with a grid on it would give him the information he needed, he wasn't close enough to read what it said, but he reckoned it was one of those wipe-over ones where what was going on was written down. He could go over there and look, but a sweep of overwhelm threatened to send him back outside. Why wasn't there a receptionist behind a desk for him to ask for help? He was on the brink of walking out when someone came out of the women's loo.

"Are you okay there?" she asked.

She didn't look official or anything, in blue jeans and a pink T-shirt, nothing fancy like he imagined a community centre manager would wear, but he liked her blonde hair and the way it hung so straight past her shoulders, and her big square glasses with black frames made her eyes seem big. Puggy wasn't sure whether he ought to speak to her or not. On the other hand, if he didn't, how was he supposed to know where to go?

He had to do this, he'd promised Miss Daulton he wouldn't run.

"I'm here for the dance class, the introductory one." It was the only dance class this evening, but he wanted to make sure she understood him and his needs.

"Oh, that's brilliant, because I'm the teacher. Come on, we're upstairs. It's through that door there."

He glanced to the left.

She tipped her head to one side. "Would you like to go first or do you want me to lead the way?"

He sagged with relief. He'd had enough of navigating his own way this evening and could do with handing the reins to her before he became overwhelmed and panicked. It bubbled just below the surface. "I'll follow you."

She pushed the door open and chatted about the weather on the way up. She was right, it was a bit warm, and he couldn't tell her he'd felt warmer than usual at home because he couldn't open the windows, not with Income in the flat. There might be noise that could carry outside. God, if he mentioned that, this woman might ask questions, and if he put his foot in it then she could phone the police. Fish and Chips would be after him then, wanting to beat him up because he'd done the wrong thing.

Life was sometimes so complicated.

On the landing, he caught his breath by a set of double doors with glass in the top. He nosed in at people throwing big darts the size of bowling pins at a Velcro board. That looked fun. How come Miss Daulton hadn't told him about that group? Maybe nobody like him went to it so she didn't think it would suit him. She'd said the main aim was for him to be himself, so it would be daft if he went and threw the darts with people he couldn't fit in with. They might laugh at him and take the piss.

The woman led him up a second flight of stairs and stopped in front of another set of double doors. "Just so you know, everyone is new here this evening, and all we'll be doing tonight is talking for half an hour, okay? Dancing starts next week. I'm sure you'll know whether you feel comfortable enough to come back, but if you'd like to give it more than five minutes before you make a decision… I'm well aware of how you might want to bolt as soon as you walk in. I'm autistic myself, it used to happen to me a lot, and it took me a long time to take control of my need to run away."

How did she know he was autistic? Had she sensed it or had Miss Daulton given her his description so she knew who he was?

"Who told you I have autism? It's a neurodivergent class, but that doesn't mean only autistic people come here."

"Very true. A couple of people have ADHD, and Sarah has Tourette syndrome. But to answer your question, I have an ism detector," she said on a laugh.

He frowned. "I don't know what you mean."

"I can spot autism in someone else a mile away."

Once he thought about it, he could see how she might be able to do that. Fish and Chips were talking about a gaydar the other day, so it must be like that, except Puggy didn't know how it worked because he didn't know if someone had autism or whether they were gay unless they told him. But would that change now, like Miss Daulton said it might? Would he learn to pick up on cues from other people like himself? He liked cues, they prompted him to remember what he was supposed to be doing next.

"Are you ready to go in?" the woman asked. "And I'm so sorry, I didn't tell you my name."

"It's Karla Beddows. It says on the leaflet you do the classes for neurodivergent people. You must be really clever if you can dance and play chess and press flowers."

She smiled. "And you'll be able to do all of them, too, if you keep coming back. The sky's the limit, that's what my mum says. What does your mum say?"

"Nothing, she's dead." Puggy hoped she wasn't offended by how blunt he'd been. Fish reckoned he was really rude when he said it how it was, but Miss Daulton said it was a part of who Puggy was and that maybe he would learn, in time, to take a pause before he gave a knee-jerk answer, and if he didn't, then that was okay.

Karla sighed. "That's sad."

"Yeah."

"Shall we go in then?"

On his way home from the community centre, Puggy couldn't stop smiling. Sometimes people said stuff to shut him up, he was sure, but Miss Daulton had been right, or her sister had. It was so much easier to sit and have a chat with people like himself, and he reckoned it wouldn't be long before he had an ism detector, too. Because he liked figuring out puzzles and spotting patterns, he'd soon picked up some of the group did certain things that he did. It was so nice to relax in front of people—that had happened almost immediately, as though he'd found a long-lost tribe.

He couldn't wait to go to the flower class tomorrow. Sarah had shouted that flower pressing was one of her most favourite things to do and that bastard daffodils and fucking shit-cunt piss-off-you-animal roses were her favourite flowers. It had taken him a few seconds to digest all of those swear words, but then she'd explained that she swore a lot when she first met people and she was really sorry if she caused any offence. Puggy was going to Google her condition later so he could understand it.

An ice cream van went past. He just fancied an orange lolly, but the van didn't stop. In the next street along, he went into the newsagent's and bought one in there, eating it as he walked.

He reckoned he had friends now. They certainly acted like them anyway, nice and chatty, and he didn't feel uncomfortable in their presence like he did with most other people. They all agreed to his suggestion of learning how to body pop and robot dance so long as he joined them in a foxtrot. He supposed he could, seeing as making friends was all about give and take. Karla had said that at the beginning when she'd chatted about what her expectations were.

"I know how easy it is to slip into wanting everything your own way because it's easier and it isn't scary if everything remains the same, but together we can hold each other's hand if it gets frightening when we're learning new things, and for those of you with a more severe panic when it comes to changing your routine, I promise that we'll all help you through it if you're feeling lost, and hopefully, all the classes will then become part of your routine without you even having to think about it."

"Fucking arsehole!" Sarah had said.

Puggy hadn't laughed like some of the others, because it wasn't Sarah's fault she said naughty things, but then *she'd* burst out laughing and said if she couldn't laugh at herself then it was a pretty wanking cock-minge life, then she'd made some weird sounds and finished with a bout of snorting.

There was so much to learn about the new people in his world, but Puggy was determined to do it. He was so lost inside his head going through everything that had happened in the meeting and didn't notice a car drawing up beside him until it was right there and someone called out through the passenger-side window. He crapped himself. What if it was Fish and Chips in their balaclavas, catching him outside when he was supposed to be indoors with Income?

But it was maybe someone worse. Two someones.

"Everything all right?"

It was George, and Puggy knew that because when he'd been confused last time they'd been round to his flat to check on him and see if he was okay, George said he'd pinch the end of his nose when he first spoke so Puggy would know who he was straight away, a helpful little signal.

Puggy had met the twins on the day they'd come to collect Shawnee, his friend. She'd been hiding from the nasty men, and when George and Greg had come to his door, he'd thought *they* were the nasty men, but they'd said they weren't, although it seemed Shawnee had thought they were. It was confusing for Puggy, but George had promised to send someone round to be his new friend, and he'd asked him if he wanted to earn pocket money from them by telling them any information he picked up from the neighbours.

He liked them, even though they were big and scary.

"Yes, thank you, George."

"Good. Been up to anything nice?"

What did that mean? Did they know he was supposed to be at home with Income? Had Fish and Chips told them what he was doing for them? Or had someone been watching his flat and let them know he'd been having visitors again? Should he tell them he'd been to the community centre? Would they tell someone about it, and that someone might tell Fish and Chips? Worry gnawed at Puggy's stomach. He didn't like it when he wasn't sure what to do.

"I just went to the shop to get a lolly."

"Yeah, we've been having nice weather, haven't we."

"Yeah."

"Has everything been okay at home?"

"Yeah."

"Any more visitors asking you to do stuff?"

"Nah."

"Can I ask you for some help?"

Puggy shrugged.

George smiled and held his phone out, showing Puggy a picture. "Do you know this woman?"

Puggy's stomach rolled over. It was Income. "She goes in the pizza shop."

"When?"

"I saw her on Friday. That's the last time I had a pizza from that shop. They were supposed to deliver it to my flat, but no one came, and when I rang them they said they didn't have my order, but I know they did because the money had been taken out of my bank. So I went down there to show them that they'd taken my money."

"And she was there."

"Yeah."

"Was she with anyone?"

"She was leaving as I was going in so I don't know."

"That's been really helpful. What about a car like this, have you seen one recently? Or more to the point, did you see one on Friday night in the car park by the shops?" George prodded his screen, bringing up Google, and tapped in a few words. He showed Puggy a picture of an old-fashioned car.

"I didn't see it." Puggy took a deep breath. George was asking too many questions, and it made him want to cut ties, to hide from him. "You're making me uncomfortable. I don't want anyone stopping me in the street or coming round. I didn't like that John you sent to be my friend, and I'd rather be by myself. I like being on my own."

"All right, mate, whatever you want, but if you change your mind then let us know."

George brought the phone inside the car and leaned forward to open the glove box. He took an envelope out and passed it to Puggy. "There's fifty quid for your trouble."

Puggy wanted it, he *always* wanted money, but what if people were watching and they knew Fish and Chips? What if they told them he'd been outside his flat? They'd know he'd left Income on her own then, *and* that he'd taken money off the twins. They might find out he was working for them on the quiet. He'd been asked to keep an eye out the front regarding the goings-on and for any gossip that the twins might want, and he had a special burner phone he had to use to contact them on. He was to send the messages, and every time he did, someone came round and posted money through his letterbox. But taking cash out in the open…

Puggy shook his head. "Can you get someone to pop it round like normal?"

"Fuck, I forgot you like things done a certain way. Sorry, and yeah, someone'll pop it round when it's dark."

"Can I go home now?"

"Yeah, and cheers for your help."

The car drove away, and Puggy hurried along the street, shitting himself in case someone had watched the whole thing. Fish and Chips had said they'd told people he worked for them, that if he even thought about working for someone else they'd find out and come round to have a go at him. Except they hadn't, so they didn't know about the twins, and he hoped they never would.

Unnerved by the unexpected chat, he rushed past the kids on the green, keeping his head down. Their ball sailed past right in front of him, but he was in no mood to pull them up on it tonight. He just wanted to get in and order a pizza from Domino's because he couldn't trust the takeaway up the road anymore.

Just as he put the key in the lock and turned it, the ball smacked him in the back of the head.

RAFFIA

Laughter erupted, and he was reduced to feeling like a child again when everyone picked on him at school. He wished his new friends from the community centre were with him now, they'd stick up for him, but they weren't and he was on his own. He stepped inside and shut the door, going to check on Income. He took the bucket away and poured the contents down the toilet, heaving at the smell. He washed it out using the showerhead, cleaned it with bleach, then took it back.

"I'm home now, and if you tap on the wall, you can use the toilet next time so long as you don't hurt me."

Income didn't speak. There was no point; his Nike socks prevented any sound from coming out. The cloth that had been in her mouth when she'd arrived had got all soggy.

"You know I'm only doing this because I'm scared of Fish and Chips."

Income's eyebrows drew together.

"Not fish and chips the dinner," he said. "The ones who were here when those men brought you. I'm scared of them."

He couldn't stand looking at her eyes any longer so shut the cupboard door then left the room, locking it behind him. In the kitchen, he washed his hands, watching the kids' football match. They'd soon fuck off if Fish and Chips turned up in their balaclavas or if the twins arrived. He wished someone would come along and frighten those boys, teach them a lesson. Maybe he could message the twins and tell them they'd thrown the ball at his head on purpose.

No, that meant they'd come round. Instead, he ordered a pizza, some chicken strips, and potato wedges. Normally that would give him two meals, but while Income was here he had to share. He didn't mind, he earned enough money for playing host, so he could afford to buy a takeaway every night if he wanted.

He stood at the window and waited for the delivery to arrive, hugging himself at the memory of how the meeting at the community centre had gone, how so much weight had dropped off his shoulders when he'd started speaking to the people there.

At last, he reckoned he could be himself.

Chapter Eight

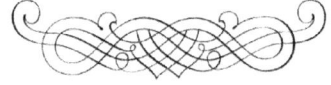

Big B hadn't smoked any more weed in the flat. He was still mellow from the last joint and had suffered an attack of conscience—or maybe it was a gut feeling and that he had the good sense not to rock any boats. He couldn't upset Floppy Tits from next door again, and the evening was too warm for him to close the balcony doors to have a smoke. Instead, he'd left the flat and now sat in a park on the grass, the shadows of trees all around him, and thought about his life and what a mess he'd made of it.

In Jamaica they worked the main road, Raffia the one who reeled the tourists in, everyone else on standby in the van in case it went wrong. The targets felt sorry for Raffia, hence why he was used—it was his bad knee and the fact that he looked like he needed food, but he was naturally skinny and could pack away a good amount without putting on weight.

At first, Big B had just been someone in the van, to fill a seat in order to make it look like the gang was bigger than it was, but then things had progressed. He'd become the person who vouched for Raffia as being someone safe, working alone in a car that he stopped at the side of the road whenever a target had been drawn into the net and was on the way towards the shops. It was all done to make it look like the target had made a good choice in allowing Raffia to guide them. Not one of them so far had turned back to the safety of the hotel, allowing the 'tour' to continue even though they were led across the street, away from the protection of passing traffic, where one of the houses could so easily belong to the gang, a place to drag the cargo into.

Back then it had seemed Big B's role was innocuous enough that he could convince himself he wasn't really doing anything wrong, but that was bullshit, especially now—now he'd proceeded up the ranks to being someone who followed the target *after* the tour scam had ended. While the little voice in the back of his head had warned him that he was progressing a *too* far, he loved the feel of dollars on his palm. They swindled up to twenty people a day, taking one target's money and then moving along the coast to do it all over again. If a target had a friend or family member with them, they got conned, too. Everyone paid through fear of being hurt. Once the van turned up and Raffia had switched from nice to nasty, everything changed.

Not everyone they chose became a different type of target. Some had been left to return to the UK and get on with their lives, while others were…

He didn't want to think about that.

In the early days they'd come close to being caught a couple of times by the Jamaican police, but the gang boss had paid them off. Now that

Big B knew exactly what the endgame was and how much money was involved, he could understand how police payments could be afforded.

Now he was here, in London, a bigger part of this than he'd ever wanted to be. This was his third time here, and he wished it could be his last, but one of the others would turn up soon, then the next leg would begin. He'd be swept up into it all, his mind on doing his part without getting caught.

He took a long drag of his joint, sifting his fingers through the cooling grass, imagining it was warm sand that fell through his fingers instead. He missed home, missed being on that private beach selling the good stuff to the guests of the hotel on the days that he wasn't used as the assuring car driver. He missed his mother who worked at the hotel in housekeeping—she'd clip him round the ear if she caught him selling to or hustling the tourists. She thought he was a good boy working at the end of the beach for Cheap Fred, whittling the cups out of bamboo.

She didn't know the half of it.

His message tone went off, and he had the urge to totally ignore it, but it could be one of the gang.

After all, he was expecting an update, and with the time difference, he calculated his mother would still be at work so it wouldn't be her.

Digby Dog: A hawk has left the nest and will arrive in the morning, UK time.

So that was it then. His short break was coming to an end. He flopped back on the grass, staring at a sky that hadn't quite got the memo that night was on the way, tinges of blue mixing in with grey. In Jamaica, the sun seemed to set in the blink of an eye: one minute the sky was bright blue and the next it was black, but here it was a gradual thing. He continued to smoke his joint, imagining a different kind of life where he didn't have the frequent need to run away and hide.

He had a sister, and he should know better — he'd kill anyone who treated Sharina the way the targets were treated. Each piece of cargo had a family who cared for them. Who cried for them. The thought of Sharina being kidnapped churned his stomach.

Big B shook his head, pushing those thoughts out of it. He studied the stars and again wished he was on the beach with the *whoosh* of the sea on the shore, the sun on his face, and the strange trilling call of the birds twittering nearby. But sometimes, no matter how hard you pretended, you just couldn't fool yourself.

He was here, in the UK, and tomorrow would be a very different day than today.

Chapter Nine

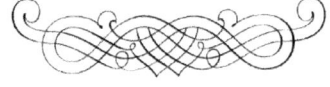

For two days after her experience with Cool Raffia, an oppressive cloud had loitered over Freya's holiday. She'd convinced herself that people from the gang freely roamed the hotel—after all, it was open-fronted, no doors or windows to stop anyone from walking into the vast reception area. And it had to be a gang, nothing could persuade her otherwise. An *organised one at that. She reckoned the van had gone off to the next hotel along the coast so they could repeat things there. How did they sleep at night? You had to be a certain person to get up every day knowing you were going to rip someone off.*

Work was being done in the foyer, some of the floor tiles switched out for new, so there was a lot of banging and sections being cordoned off. The men doing that work could be anyone. They didn't have uniforms like the other staff. Her overactive imagination told her that Cool Raffia had sent them to find her, so she'd taken to wearing a floppy sunhat, stuffing her hair underneath it, and avoiding wearing the clothes she'd had on the other day. She'd become jumpy and anxious, never sharing the lift with anyone; if it stopped on another floor for someone to get in, she got out and waited for another. Too cautious? If the gate guards weren't bothered and the rep was making out she knew nothing about such scams, then maybe they were all in on it, so it was best she stayed vigilant.

But enough of letting it ruin her time away. Freya had woken up telling herself off. While she'd been tricked and it was horrible, and it had left a scar she was sure would always be there, the gang was off fleecing someone else. They'd remain in her mind forever, but she was probably already erased from theirs. She was likely one in a long line of people who'd been conned into handing their money over, nothing special.

With her swimming costume on underneath a short floaty dress, her beach bag hanging from her shoulder, she headed to the buffet for breakfast. Despite telling herself to stop being so silly, she automatically scanned the faces of everyone sitting on the open terrace eating their food, but none of them resembled Cool Raffia or the man in the car.

Pack it in.

She shut her mind off from what had happened and entered the buffet. The line for the cooked breakfast was always so long, so she chose croissants again as well as a cinnamon whirl and some melon. She had ten days out of fourteen left and, determined to enjoy herself— as much as she could while holidaying alone, something she'd never done before—she took her plate into the indoor eating section and waited for one of the staff to ask her what she wanted to drink. Coffee, it would always be coffee at this time of day.

When the woman came back bearing a tray, Freya asked, "Do you know Cool Raffia?"

The server's face scrunched up.

She does know him, or she's at least heard of him.

"I don't, my lady."

That was another thing Freya had noticed, how most Jamaicans addressed people so nicely, and it wasn't just because they were being paid to either; at the airport, someone on the same flight had called Freya "my lady" when she'd apologised for bumping into her.

"Perhaps don't leave the resort." The server poured Freya's drink then placed down the usual little metal jug of hot, frothy milk. She popped the coffee pot on the table and walked away.

Unless Freya was completely mistaken, Cool Raffia's name was known around here. Maybe he was the local shitbag. If the same thing went on here as it did in England, you grew up in a certain area and got to know who the bad boys and girls were, and even when you were an adult and hadn't seen them for years, you still remembered them. The server's warning that Freya shouldn't leave the resort had come a bit too late but was appreciated, nonetheless. Had she been warned not to leave for a reason? As in the gang had a next level that they acted out on holidaymakers? She hadn't even told her not to go alone, so did that mean they preyed on groups, too?

Freya ate her breakfast then went off to find a shaded space on the beach. Although there were a lot of palm trees to sit under, you had to be early to secure a bed. Thankfully, she'd gone into breakfast at half past seven, and with it being above twenty-six degrees even overnight, it was already warm enough to sunbathe.

She dragged away the second bed so it was clear she wanted to be by herself, then changed her mind and put it back. She placed her sunhat on it, plus her bag, so it would look like someone else had gone off for a swim and would come back to join her shortly. A few of the male staff here had given her suggestive looks and called her "pretty baby", something she wouldn't have thought would be allowed to happen. Speaking to the guests like that wasn't exactly proper, was it. Just last night, the singer from the house reggae band had flirted with several women when he'd walked down from the stage to sing with them on the dance floor. She supposed some people would like that, but she didn't. After all, the reason she was here all by herself was because of flirting.

She hadn't yet taken the time on this holiday to sift through everything that had happened prior to coming here. She'd already been through the betrayal numerous times before and after her split with James, but the lead-up to it, what she'd completely missed…she hadn't gone through that in great detail because it meant accepting she'd being duped for months. James had admitted that what he'd engaged in could be seen as a full-blown affair with a work colleague, but he'd insisted he hadn't seen it as such, just that they were mates.

An "emotional" affair they called it these days, where you were with someone in everything other than actually having sex. For some reason James had given Theresa his phone number and she'd been contacting him on WhatsApp out of office hours during the week. Memes that related to their working life, little jokes between them regarding their boss. The messages had then come over the weekend, and one night, when Freya had turned over onto her other side, she'd seen his phone screen over his shoulder. Theresa had sent a goodnight text with a love heart. James had quickly put his phone under the covers and then moved onto his *other side to face Freya. When he brought is mobile out again, she couldn't see anything. If that wasn't suspicious, she didn't know what was, and she'd called him out on it right there and then.*

Of course, he'd come up with the excuse that everyone used love hearts these days, it didn't mean anything, and that if he was doing something out of order with Theresa, he wouldn't be so stupid as to keep the same passcode that opened his phone. She'd retorted that he'd kept it because he'd known she wouldn't snoop, she wasn't the type—she didn't even know whether it was the same code as he'd told her because until then she'd never had reason to doubt him enough to use it.

And she'd thought he wasn't the kind of man to speak to a female work colleague when his working day had ended because he'd once said that kind of thing was disrespectful to a partner and gave them cause to think the worst, yet there he was…

Tears stung Freya's eyes. Glad she had sunglasses on to hide them, she settled back and stared at the blue sky, the puffy white clouds, and the sway of the palm tree branches. James had been the one person in the whole world she'd thought would never do this to her. She'd laughed whenever anyone had asked her if she trusted him completely, because she did. Had. The things he'd said in the past, sincerely and with conviction, had persuaded her that cheating was not on his agenda, ever, in any form. Okay, he may well not have taken that final step with Theresa, but he'd still been unfaithful. Needing another a woman for emotional support and flirting when you already had someone who gave you everything you could need…then again, Freya obviously hadn't, had she. If she'd been the perfect partner, then none of this would have happened.

But she wasn't going to go down the road of blaming herself again. It was James who'd allowed the messaging to become so frequent, to cross the line into flirting—admittedly it was only on Theresa's part to begin with; Freya had seen all the messages when he'd shown her later that night. But it was James who hadn't said, "Hang on a minute, I'm in a relationship, and what you just sent me isn't appropriate..."

He'd said he'd felt awkward at the thought of telling Theresa to back off because he worked with her so closely, and that told Freya all she needed to know. He didn't care enough about her to risk losing his job if he spoke out to his boss or HR. Yes, men were usually the predators, but even Freya could see that Theresa had set out to draw James in. But he hadn't been innocent in all of this. He'd sent laughing emojis or winks whenever she'd said anything Freya considered a bit too far. James had said he didn't know what else to respond with. How about: Err, fuck off.

And that was why Freya had ended it. Had she been in James's position, she wouldn't have given a shit about upsetting the apple cart at work. She wouldn't have given a colleague her private phone number in the first place.

Now, here she was, on a sunbed in the Caribbean, two weeks after she'd last spoken to James and they'd split up, contemplating the hurt and trying to stop herself from imagining putting her hands around Theresa's neck.

The most infuriating thing about it all was that Theresa had a little boy and a husband, so what had she been playing at?

Freya got her Kindle out. She didn't want to think about that anymore. She had her future to plan before she went home, but not today. Today she'd spend it reading, napping, and eating, and tonight she'd watch the show on offer, a mini musical called At the Train Station, *which started at eight. She hadn't stayed up past ten o'clock here, because the resort was so big and with so many guests that she found it overwhelming once people had drunk too much. Besides, by then she was desperate for the coldness of her room.*

She read a couple of chapters and then popped her Kindle in her bag, holding the handles to prevent theft while she closed her eyes for a moment. Not that she'd seen anybody take anything, and people openly left their stuff on the sunbeds to either go in the sea or the pools, but knowing her luck, she'd be the one to have her belongings nicked.

She could have napped or she could have been awake all this time, she didn't know, but something blocked the light, turning the insides of her eyelids darker. She snapped her eyes open. A man in a white shirt and black trousers stood staring down at her, his short dreads neat and tidy, his beard trimmed nice.

"Do you want to go on the pedalos, use a paddleboard, or go to Dunn's River, my lady? I can give you a discount for the river. It's supposed to be one hundred and ten dollars for adults, but I'll take you for ninety. It's on the catamaran over there. Drinks are free. There's a stop at a secluded beach for an hour, and another stop at the shopping centre. You have to pay twenty-five dollars to get into Dunn's River on top."

"No thank you," she said. "I don't want to leave the resort."

"It's safe with us. We work in conjunction with the hotel. I'm Mr P."

"No, I'm okay, thank you."

He scribbled on a notepad that he'd taken from his trouser pocket, ripped off the top sheet, and handed it to her as though she hadn't told him — twice — that she wasn't interested. She stopped herself from barking out a negative response and took the paper.

"The discount is only valid until tomorrow," he called out and walked away.

She was nowhere near a bin so popped the paper in her bag and took her Kindle out again. Just one day, that's all she wanted, where she wasn't approached by someone who wanted her money.

She managed to read for another half an hour before someone else came up to her. A man in Jamaican colours from his hat to his T-shirt to his shorts to his flip-flops. She sat up, swinging her legs around so her feet rested on the sand, then she pushed herself up and packed her things away. It was pointless staying here if she was going to keep being bothered.

"Want to buy some souvenirs for your friends and family back home?"

"No thank you." She slid her sandals on.

"There are some nice things down the other end of the beach made by Cheap Fred."

"I've already bought things from Fred."

"And you had the tour."

She stopped in the act of picking up her bag, bent over as she was to reach for it on the other sunbed. Her stomach rolled over, her chest going tight, and a shot of fear went through her. She glanced ahead at other bathers, but none of them were looking her way. Then anger took place of the fear, and she straightened, turning to stare at this new man.

"How do you know I had the tour?"

"The guards at the gate were talking about it."

He raised his hands to show her he meant no harm. Had there been a security camera on the outside of the little hut? Had they discussed her and watched the footage? Otherwise, how else would he know who she was? Unless one of the men in the van had taken a picture of her…

No, she was being really silly now.

"How did you know it was me?" She clutched her bag handles tight, the strawlike material digging into her skin.

He shrugged. "The guard pointed you out this morning."

"I was nowhere near the hut for him to have done that."

"No, it was when he turned up for work. We have to sign in, at reception. You walked past when you got out of the lift, that's all."

"Why did you even bring it up, that I had the tour?"

"Because you need to be careful. Don't go out of here again unless you're on the tour operator bus, do you understand?"

She nodded, her mind jumping to so many scenarios it wasn't funny. Why hadn't he told her about that straight off the bat? Why bring up Cheap Fred first?

She asked him that.

"I had to make sure I had the right person. Keep away from Cool Raffia. Be careful when you go home, too."

What?

He strode away across the sand, approaching a couple, talking to them and then pointing towards the end of the beach, so he must be a tout for the Cheaps down there but just so happened to have warned her to keep safe.

Should she approach the rep again? Make a proper complaint? Let her know that other staff members knew about the tour and the scam and that something ought to be done about Cool Raffia being allowed to hang around up there by the guard hut, waiting to pounce on innocent people?

She walked to the steps that led to the long balcony and decided to sit at one of the tables and write an email to the tour operator direct. She had a feeling she'd get nowhere with the rep. She'd compose it now and save it as a draft, sending it once she got home and she was completely safe. She felt it best to listen to her gut instinct that was telling her she wasn't *safe here, not even on the resort that had security guards who patrolled all of the areas.*

RAFFIA

For all she knew, one of them could be best friends with the gang members.

Chapter Ten

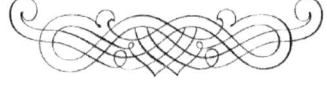

James Pratt lived in a flat above a vape shop. The area was kind of a no-man's-land between housing estates. It would be a good five-minute walk from any of the nearby homes. The little parade of shops backed onto a playing field which the twins had driven past on their way here. The boys fucking about playing football reminded George of being a kid himself, and the two lads and a little girl sitting together on the grass gave him a serious case of the memories. George and Greg having a picnic with Gail, the girl they'd grown up thinking was their best friend but she was really their half-sister. They didn't see much of her these days, and George knew damn well it was because he didn't want the truth accidentally slipping out of his big mouth. Gail would be devastated to know that Ron Cardigan had been with her mother, but she'd be pleased as punch to know she was related to The Brothers. She'd always said there was a connection between them that she couldn't explain.

On the street outside the shops, George and Greg stood in front of a black door with a slightly wonky number seven on it, not enough for most people to notice, but with George being so anal, it stood out to him. The knocker was set on one of those vertical letterboxes, silver, and he gave it a tap. And kept tapping until footsteps thudded behind the door and it opened. A slender man with floppy blond hair looked at them, his expression saying it all. He knew who they were in their grey suits and red ties and wasn't about to give them any hassle. Good. Always a bonus, that.

"James Pratt?" George asked, less of the menace, more the tone of someone asking nicely. While it seemed this man had no intention of playing up, that might change if George acted belligerent. It put some people's backs up.

"Yes…"

"Can we have a word, please?" *You can't say fairer than that, can you? I even said please.*

James didn't seem to know what to do with his arms. Cross them and he'd look either defensive or dodgy, but let them hang by his sides and he might not be able to defend himself in time should a fist come flying his way. "Um, yeah, but what's it about?"

"Freya."

His eyebrows rose. "What about her?"

George glanced left and right. No one was around, but the little newsagent's on the end was still open, as was the chip shop, so people could appear at any moment. "We'd prefer to talk inside."

James shrugged and led the way up the stairs. It was carpeted nice, and the fresh smell of paint lingered from where the landlord must have given the walls a go-over before offering the place to James. On the landing, he turned right through a doorway that had a Yale lock on it, extra security if someone broke in via the main door on the street. George strode into a living room and stood beside James who looked out of the window onto the road. Someone had parked outside and currently legged it across into the newsagent's. Greg came in and closed the door, eyeing the place, an open-plan living room and kitchen with two doors off to the left, likely leading to a bedroom and bathroom.

"Anyone else at home?" George asked.

"No. Please don't hurt me."

George took his attention away from an Uber Eats man on his bike going to the chip shop. James shook, his bottom lip quivering. What kind of fella was he to have let them in if he thought they were going to hurt him? Was he a 'roll over and rub my belly' type? Did he think that if they planned to do him some damage then it was pointless fighting it?

George felt sorry for the poor bastard. "Listen, we're not in the habit of hurting anyone if they don't deserve it. You've got nothing to worry about, providing you haven't done anything to Freya—"

"Hang on, what?" James whipped his head round and stared at George.

Going by his face, he genuinely didn't know what was going on.

"I'll start at the beginning," George said on a sigh. "Freya hasn't been seen or made contact with her mother or her friend, Lottie, since Friday night. The last sighting we know about is when she left the pizza shop down near where she lives and walked towards her flat. We've got our CCTV man looking for where she went after that, to see if she even made it home, but there's no sign in her gaff of the pizza box or the bottle of wine and sweets she purchased. Now, she could have tidied up, and those things could be in a communal bin out the back, but none of the neighbours recall seeing her return from the shops. That's not to say she didn't come back, just that they didn't see her. There's something we haven't told her mother yet because we don't want to scare her unnecessarily, she's in a bad enough state as it is, but two men were caught on camera staring after her when she began her walk home from the pizza shop."

"Bloody hell... I warned her about walking on her own. That's why she always got taxis home from work because I insisted."

"But you're not with her anymore to look after her, are you."

James winced.

George continued. "They didn't drive off after her straight away, they had a chat amongst themselves, so going off in her direction may well be a massive coincidence, but they drove an old-fashioned Jaguar S Type, and it wasn't in the best of nick. Do you know anyone who owns a car like that? Dark in colour?"

"No."

"As you can imagine, Maria's pretty worried, and the police are doing fuck all, God bless their useless souls."

"Why aren't they?"

"It's the usual shite, where they've brushed Maria's concerns aside. To be fair to them, have you seen all the appeals that go up on Facebook for missing people on the local plod page, then two hours later that person's found? They've got their work cut out for them trying to figure out which people are actually in danger and which ones are just off living their lives. Anyway, *we're* looking for her."

Greg came over and leaned on the windowsill. "What would you say if Freya sent you a text telling you to back off because you were getting on her nerves?"

James reared his head back as if surprised, although his eyebrows told another story—that he was confused. "It's not something she'd say."

Greg pinched the bridge of his nose. "See, this is what Maria and Lottie said, but surely Freya got arsey from time to time. Like when she found out you were cheating, for instance."

James flinched, and his eyes watered as though the subject of him cheating brought him pain. A pink flush crawled up his neck to mottle his jawline. Now that Greg had fired his arrow and hit the mark, he buggered off to the other side of the room, leaving George to deal with any fallout.

Penis.

James glanced at George briefly and then down at the carpet. "No, she wasn't even angry then, just quietly spoken and hurt. She barely ever raised her voice at me. It wasn't that she didn't get annoyed because she did sometimes, me leaving dirty washing on the floor, stuff like that, but she didn't shout about it, she just asked me not to do it anymore."

"So it's definitely out of character for her to send a message like that," George asked.

James stared out of the window again. "Yes, she just wouldn't have done it, especially to her mum. They're really close. Freya's got too much respect for her to say anything cutting. She wouldn't say boo to a goose usually."

"So is she a bit of a wet blanket, a walkover?"

"God, no, she just doesn't like hurting people's feelings or causing offence." James ran both hands through his hair then held the back of his neck as though to anchor himself in place. "What do you think's going on?"

George pinched his chin. "The men with the Jaguar aside, she could have just fucked off for the weekend and decided to stay away until this evening."

"Why this evening?"

"She's got work tomorrow, as you probably know, so she could pop up any minute. We've got a man stationed outside her flat to watch for if she comes home, and our coppers are having a discreet poke into whether she's used her bank cards recently."

"Why does it have to be discreet?"

"It just does. If she hasn't spent any money since she bought the pizza, then that's bloody telling."

"Why? She could be using cash."

"True—if it's normal for her to withdraw it and keep some in her purse. Is it?"

"No."

"So why suggest she might use cash then?"

"I don't *know*!" James looked like he might cry. "I'm trying to help by offering answers."

"News has come in that she had an unhappy incident in Jamaica. I asked her mum and Lottie to see if they know what it's about, but according to them, Freya never told them anything bad about the holiday. Despite you two splitting up, did she confide in you about it by any chance?"

"I didn't even know she'd *gone* to Jamaica. She never said a word about it when we arranged for what day and time I could go there to collect my stuff."

"How were things left with you two?"

"She was really hurt, obviously, and couldn't stand to even look at me."

"When was the last time you had contact with her?"

"Even though I'd written a note and left it in her flat, I sent her a message to reiterate that I'd put the keys on the side in the kitchen and if there was any of my stuff left behind, if she could let me know then I'd arrange to have it picked up." He took his phone out of his pocket and opened WhatsApp, scrolling for Freya's name and showing George the screen full of messages.

Satisfied with what he was reading, George still scrolled up to see if there had been any contact while Freya had been in the Caribbean. Maybe that was the unhappy incident that had happened, they'd had a row or something, but no, prior to the message about the key were ones regarding how sorry James was and he wished he could make it up to her, so George assumed that was after she'd found out what he'd done with the other woman. Before that was the usual domestic stuff about grabbing a loaf and did he want to go out for dinner because she didn't feel like cooking.

That saddened George. One minute her life had been fine, her mind on nothing but bread, the next James had become an ex who'd begged for her forgiveness—messages she'd ignored.

How quickly life changed.

"Who were you having it away with?" George asked.

"I wasn't having it away with anyone. Freya called it an emotional affair. I called it talking to my work wife."

"That term says it all, you absolute fanny. It implies she's your wife in every way apart from the bedroom. Do you realise how upsetting that would be for Freya if you'd ever used that term in front of her?"

"I didn't think of it like that."

"Seems you didn't think at all," Greg muttered.

"So, who is she?" George asked.

"Theresa Scrivens."

George took the liberty of looking at those messages, too. It was obvious James had got some balls and told her they weren't to flirt anymore, even though he and Freya had split by that point. The messages from the past looked like Theresa had been the instigator. The memes she'd sent where a little risqué sometimes.

"See that, there?" George stabbed a finger in the air above one of the images with the caption: WHEN YOU LOOK AT YOUR WORK WIFE ACROSS THE ROOM AND KNOW EXACTLY WHAT SHE'S THINKING.

"Right at that point was when you should have said she'd gone below the belt."

"I don't understand why that particular meme is wrong."

"It implies intimacy, not necessarily sexual, just that you're close enough to know what the other is thinking in certain situations. This sort of thing could really make someone feel insecure, so no wonder Freya called it an emotional affair."

"I know that now, I just didn't want to make any waves at work by telling Theresa to pack it in."

"So you chose to continue allowing your colleague to flirt with you, knowing that at any time your girlfriend might see what was going on? What did you think, that what she didn't know wouldn't hurt her?"

"Put like that, it sounds really bad."

"And if you're being honest, you quite liked the attention."

"I suppose that must have been it, but I never would have cheated on Freya. If things looked like they were going to another level with Theresa I would have ended things with Freya first. As it was, she found out and ended it anyway. She said she could never trust me again, even though I hadn't *really* stepped over the line, and I had to accept that."

"Very noble of you." George rolled his eyes. "Is there anyone Freya might have upset, someone she'd have to hide from for a few days?"

"God, no. Freya wouldn't do anything to hurt anyone."

"What's she like with money? Could she owe rent and that's why she's fucked off so she can work out how to get her finances straight?"

"Everything's on direct debit, and there's always enough money in her bank. As long as I've known her she's had savings, and there's no way she'd pay out on a holiday if she couldn't afford it. There's no way on this earth she wouldn't have paid her rent."

"So we're talking a disappearance in dodgy circumstances or she's gone away and not told anyone."

"I can't see her doing that either—the not telling anyone. She talks to her mum every day. It's one of the things I didn't like about her. I must have been jealous or something, you know, those messages to Maria meant it was less time she spent focusing on me. I felt excluded."

"Oh, and you thought it was okay to do the same back by messaging Theresa, even though you knew how it felt to be *excluded*? Next you'll be telling me you were neglected by Freya and that's why you turned to Theresa."

James didn't answer that one.

George nosed out into the street. The Uber Eats biker was long gone, but a row of three cars had parked in front of the BMW. Someone came out of the chippy and got into the front car, driving away. It took all of a minute, that was all, but a minute was a long time when no one was speaking.

"What have you been up to since Friday night?" George asked.

James puffed out some air as though he'd been waiting for that question, but he didn't appear to have any problem answering it. "Friday I was down the Noodle with a couple of mates until closing, then I kipped round one of their places to save me walking all the way back here. We went to football Saturday, and yesterday I was round my mum's for dinner—my nan's up from Bournemouth, so I spent some time with her. Today I've been at work. What, do you think I've done away with Freya? Check the other rooms, she's not in them, and I'll give you the addresses and phone numbers of my mates and my mum, and my job if you need it. I've got nothing to hide."

Greg walked off through one of the doorways, and James recited the information. George put it in his notes app. Greg came out of the bedroom and entered the other doorway, returning with a shrug and a shake of his head.

"Will you let me know when you find her?" James said. "I still love her to death, and I hate the thought of something horrible happening to her."

"Are you hoping to get back together with her?" George asked.

"Yeah." James got misty-eyed. "I thought we'd get married and have kids, you know?"

"Sucks to be you." George patted him on the back. "If you hear from her or see her, let us know." He took a business card out of his pocket and handed it over. "We'll see ourselves out."

Once they were settled in the car, George let out a long breath. "Fucking dead ends everywhere. Break it down for me so I can get it straight in my head because it's all a bloody jumble at the minute."

Greg tutted. "I'm not your personal assistant."

"Stop being a dickhead and just help me out."

Greg sighed. "We've got Bennett on the CCTV and Anaisha on Freya's financials. Colin's looking at the footage from the takeaway shop, and Mason's having a poke around to see if he can find anything out about her time in Jamaica. We ought to go to the Noodle and ask a few questions there, seeing as that's where she usually drinks."

George nodded. "Come on then. I can have a Pot Noodle and some tiger bread while we're there."

"Bloody hell, we've not long had a burger and chips."

George patted his stomach. "Human dustbin, me."

In her office, Nessa, the manager of the Noodle, recognised Freya's picture straight away. Of course she did. That was why the twins had employed her because she was so good at storing faces in that brain of hers—faces and incidents and gossip and God knew what else. She sat behind her desk with her feet up on top of it. She worked her arse off, and although she took regular holidays at George's insistence, it was clear she wasn't getting proper rest.

"Before we dive into things," George said, "if you don't mind me saying, you look like a bag of shit."

"What do you mean, if I don't mind you saying? You wouldn't give a toss whether I minded anyway."

"Fair point. Do you need to get yourself down the doctor's? Or we can send you to a private clinic."

"It's nothing for you to worry about and it's all in hand."

"Tell us anyway."

She closed her eyes for a second, pushed out a long breath, then stared him straight in the eye. "Perimenopause."

"Ah."

She raised her eyebrows at him. "Do you still want to talk about it?"

"If it makes you feel better."

"Not really. All you need to know is that I'm on HRT and I'm starting to feel less like I want to stab people in the face."

"I can't imagine feeling like that because I quite enjoy wanting to stab people in the face. Why didn't you tell us?"

"I didn't let anyone know what was going on. I went to work and did what I had to do, so on the outside it looked like everything was the same, but inside, there was a stranger living there. I felt like I was going mental to be honest. If I could have curled into a ball and hidden from the world, I would have done. It came on really quickly, too. One minute I was the normal Nessa, then the next I wasn't. I wasn't myself at all, and I can't explain it very well, but it was like a huge chunk of me had been erased and I didn't know how to get it back again. I couldn't even remember what that chunk was like, and it scared me, like I had to get to know this new person I'd become. My confidence was shot, I couldn't sleep yet I was exhausted…"

"You should have said. We'd have tried to help."

"Like I just told you, I actually thought I was going mental, properly insane, the kind where you get put in a special hospital, so talking about it was the last thing I wanted to do. I was paranoid someone would section me. It wasn't until I couldn't take it anymore that I went to the doctor and blurted it all out. Hormones have got a lot to answer for."

"Shit a brick. You women have to put up with so much crap."

"Yeah, well, the pills I'm taking have worked wonders, and there's this gel I have to rub in. Now if the waking up at night with hot sweats would just fuck off, I'd be totally back to normal again."

"Do you need some time off?"

"If I do, I'll take it."

Mindful of how Nessa may be feeling now that she'd confessed some of her deepest feelings to them, George would tread carefully with her. It really bothered him that she'd felt so vulnerable, and with no one to talk to—she'd chosen that, but still, the idea of her suffering alone and trying to muddle on through her life, he felt sorry for her. It wasn't easy to admit you thought you were actually going crazy.

I should know, been there and done that.

He had the urge to go over to her and scoop her up in a hug, but knowing her as he did, she wouldn't appreciate it, not outwardly anyway, and he didn't want to embarrass her.

Nessa took her feet off the table and scooted her chair forward. Back to business, then. "You mentioned Freya Duncan. I suppose you're here to ask me what I know about her. Not an awful lot if I'm honest. She usually comes in over the weekend with her fella, James I think his name is, although she hasn't been in with him for a while. I heard they'd split up—I was earwigging when she was last in here with her friend, Lottie Jacobs. James was in here on Friday night with a couple of friends, Aiden and Oliver."

George nodded. "The same names as he gave us."

"So you've asked him for an alibi if he's giving you his mates' names. Am I allowed to know what's gone on, because I can't imagine for the life of me that any of those three would be up to no good. They're all a bit...nerdy, for want of a better word."

"Straight-laced, good boys?"

"Yes, that's them. It stands out a mile they haven't got the balls to do anything bad. So like I said, what's gone on?"

"Freya's either buggered off for a long weekend or something's happened to her." George explained about the out-of-character text message and Maria's gut feeling that something was wrong. He went on to tell her about the CCTV outside the takeaway and the broken vase. "None of it proves anything sinister has happened, but it's going to bug me just the same until we find her."

"I wish I could help you. The last time I saw her she'd just got back from Jamaica and she popped in here with Lottie. Tuesday last week. If she was in after that then I didn't see her. I had Wednesday and Thursday off and spent it in my bed reading books and getting the chef to bring food up to my flat on demand."

"Bloody good for you, and I mean that," George said, "no sarcasm in sight. You do whatever you need to in order to make yourself feel better. Do you need a cuddle or anything?"

Her eyes filled. "Sodding hell, I'm only ever seconds away from crying at the best of times, and it's bloody hard work trying to stop it, so while I appreciate your offer, I'm not going to take you up on it, because once I start crying, I don't think I'm going to stop."

"Sometimes it's good to cry like that. Doesn't mean you're weak." George left that particular conversation there—the look on her face told him she'd all of a sudden got the urge to be stabby again. "Can you keep your ear to the ground for us? The second Freya walks in, we want to know about it."

"Of course."

George led the way out of the office and helped himself to a latte from the self-serve coffee machine on the bar. He'd put his order in for a Pot Noodle before they'd spoken to Nessa, and a server looked for him now, his and Greg's food on a tray. George beckoned him over to a spare table.

"Cheers."

The server walked away, and George got on with dipping buttered tiger bread in his noodle sauce while he waited for Greg who chatted to someone at the bar, likely asking about Freya.

This might not be anything, her not answering her phone.

But it could be something, and because of that, his mind wouldn't rest until he'd found out what, if anything, was going on.

Chapter Eleven

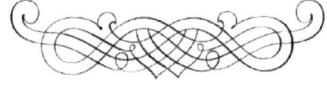

Colin had received a copy of the CCTV footage via an email address he kept specifically for his dealings with the twins. Once upon a time he'd been a straight-as-a-die copper who'd never put a foot wrong if he could help it, and now, here he was, using VPNs on the dark web, looking shit up at work using other people's login details, and willingly breaking the law in order to achieve what The Brothers wanted—which was justice, but they didn't necessarily get it the legal way, and he was okay with that now. Since his wife had been murdered, he didn't view the world the same way, and he was okay with *that*, too.

He'd come to learn that life wasn't always black and white, right or wrong, and he shook his head at himself for ever thinking that was the case. He'd previously thought of the twins as degenerates, men who enjoyed going around hurting people for fun, but they were nothing like that. It had taken him a few months to come to terms with who he'd turned into. How he could behave like his old self at work, good old Colin on the outside but a monster on the inside. Some of the thoughts he had these days weren't fit for human consumption, so he kept them to himself, but if there ever came a time when he had to let them out, there was his ex-colleague, Janine, and of course the twins who he could chat to. Speaking of Janine, he'd go and see her later. She always put everything into perspective.

They kept in regular contact via WhatsApp, and she'd said earlier that her boyfriend, Cameron, was out this evening on a job for the twins—and by the sound of it, it was nothing to do with the Freya Duncan case. Colin could go round there, have a cuppa with her, something he did begrudgingly (the cuppa, not visiting her) because he'd rather be drinking Pepsi Max. Janine reckoned he ought to stop necking so much of it, and he reckoned she should mind her own business.

He clicked the icon to open one of the attachments and let the short clip of footage play out. There were two sides to the story on the screen.

1: Freya had left the takeaway and headed for home, two men watching her go by. Nothing sinister.

2: Freya had left the takeaway and headed for home, the two men had discussed her, then followed in their car. Something had happened to her.

The thing was, if that were true, then they had to know her address before they'd seen her at the takeaway. The time it had taken between them watching her and going after her was too long for them to catch up, even in a car. She would have reached home before they'd even left the car park.

If it was a case of them keeping her under surveillance, which could be why they were at the parade of shops, why was she being watched? Had the ex-boyfriend sent them to keep an eye on her?

Colin typed that thought into a message.

GG: We don't think he's dodgy, he didn't give us that impression, but looks and actions can be deceiving, so the jury's out on that one. Then again, we spoke to Nessa, and she's of the opinion that James isn't the type to have done anything to Freya. There must be another reason why she may have been watched.

Colin: I'm sure something will come to light eventually.

He clicked on another icon to open the second attachment. The time at the top of the screen showed the footage was from much earlier on. She walked towards the parade alone, along the path beside the car park, then went out of shot where she must have entered the newsagent's. George had already given him details of her movements when he'd sent the email.

A Jaguar S Type drew into the car park from the direction of Freya's flat and pulled into an empty space—the same space it was in on the other clip. Colin sped things up a little, slowing it back down to real time when Freya left the pizza place.

No part of her demeanour suggested she was afraid.

Back when Colin had started working for the twins, he'd have felt the need to tell someone at work about this footage and the suspicion that Freya had come a cropper. It would have burrowed into his conscience that officers ought to be out there doing the legwork on this, not the twins and their men, but despite the resources at the police's disposal, the twins had a habit of getting results a lot faster. If it looked to Colin as though they were being met by too many dead ends, he'd suggest they speak to Freya's mother and urge her to contact her local station again.

His phone rang, which didn't surprise him at all as he'd been expecting either George or Greg to give him a ring, but what *did* surprise him was to see the name MASON on the screen, the twins' private detective.

"Hello?" Colin answered.

"George told me to get hold of you."

"Okay."

"I've had a deep dive into a few threads online."

"Right…"

"There's a forum that's discussing people going missing in the same area but the police not putting two and two together that they're linked. For example, this family has been campaigning to keep their son's disappearance in the public eye because the police have said all leads have dried up. The parents aren't willing to put up and shut up, as there are five men of around the same age who went missing in the same circumstances — walking home from a night out, and all of them had sent messages to family members to say they would be home soon. Clearly, none of them had any intention of taking themselves off somewhere."

"Where is all this going on?"

"Bristol."

"So what's that got to do with Freya?"

"Nothing, it's just an example of what I'm about to tell you next. It's things that have similarities in common that's bothering me. Someone put up a response on one of the threads to say that their cousin went on holiday to Jamaica at the beginning of March, and a week after she returned she went missing. The comment then went on to say that they'd discovered *other* UK women had also been to Jamaica and were missing, all just by trawling Facebook after putting Jamaica in the search bar."

"Shit."

"Exactly, so what the twins want to know is whether you can access the database and pop in the word Jamaica and see what comes up."

"I can but I'm not at work at the moment. Anaisha is, though."

"Will you pass the information on to her and ask her to do it?"

"Yep."

"Thanks."

Mason ended the call, leaving Colin to stare at the footage where he'd paused it—Freya being watched by the men standing by the car. Using his burner, he messaged Anaisha to let her know what was needed. He closed the footage windows, logged out of this email, shut down the browser, and lowered the lid of his laptop. He got up and took a Pepsi Max out of the fridge to drink on the way to Janine's—and that reminded him to send her a message to check if it was okay that he went round. She might be putting little Rosie to bed round about now, and he didn't want to disturb their routine by just turning up.

JANINE: YEP, THE PRINCESS IS IN BED, AND I'M BORED, PLUS I'M INTRIGUED AS TO WHAT'S GOING ON WITH YOU AT THE MOMENT. I'LL PUT THE KETTLE ON. [WINK EMOJI]

COLIN: DO YOU HAVE TO?

JANINE: [ROW OF SMILING EMOJIS]

Colin was about to respond when his phone rang, Anaisha's name on the screen.

"Did you find anything out?" he asked as soon as he accepted the call.

"Bloody hell, give me a chance!" She spoke quietly, probably because she was still at work. "On the one hand I'm surprised that this hasn't been picked up on before, and on the other, I'm not, because women going missing after they've been to Jamaica maybe isn't something the officers would have thought happened often, therefore, they wouldn't have searched up on it…"

Colin's stomach rolled over. Shit, this was sounding serious. "How many women are we talking?"

"Eight, nine with Freya."

"Fuck."

"You know as well as I do that if this case came our way we'd probably think it was a one-off and her previously being on holiday was nothing to do with it. Plus there's the fact that the women have gone missing at different places in the country. If they were all going missing from the same area then that commonality would be more likely to stick out to investigating officers in the missing person's team, but as they haven't…"

"Hmm, but even then nothing may have been done." He told her about the disappearances in Bristol and how the police there hadn't seemed to pick up on any links.

"Bloody hell, or they *have* twigged but they're keeping it quiet in case it sets the public off thinking there's a serial killer out there or at the very least someone kidnapping people."

"Or they just haven't made the connection."

"Wow." She tapped something, the sound tinny and annoying. "So regarding Freya. Now that there's a potential link with the other women going missing after going to Jamaica, what are we going to do about it?"

"We tell the twins and leave it at that."

"But… I've done the search using someone else's details, of course, which just happens to be the officer Freya's mother spoke to. I chose him on purpose because he's on the front desk. I've had his login info for ages. It won't seem odd that he'd have looked up the word Jamaica after he'd spoken to Freya's mother, but it *will* look odd that he hasn't done anything about it—he'd have got the same results I did. Normally there'd be a follow-up to the mother regarding what he'd discovered. I don't feel right him possibly getting in the shit for not doing that."

"You could make a note in the file that he contacted her about it."

"But that's not going to make the Jamaica connection go away, is it. The mum would expect him to investigate it, speak to all the other families who have people missing." She sighed. "Sometimes, I fucking hate working for the twins. When this sort of crap happens, and an innocent person could get accused of not doing their job properly because I used their login, it's just so bloody wrong."

Colin felt the same as she did. He'd never liked using other people's identities to gain information, but what else could they do? "Is there any way you can have a chat with the officer on the desk?"

"Like what?"

"Make out your mum knows her mum, Maria, and that she said Freya hasn't made contact since Friday, so you wondered whether he could help by looking into it." He thought of something and slapped his forehead. "Forget that, because if he starts poking around regarding Jamaica, you searching in his name would crop up, bringing attention to it, which is something we don't want. The best bet is for me to speak to the twins and explain that if Freya has been taken by persons unknown, then this needs to be dealt with under the radar so that the search on the police computer can just die a death."

"Okay, I'll leave that with you."

He placed the phone on the table and stood for a moment, digesting the information. The policeman in him wanted to open up a case, get justice for all the other people who'd gone missing, give their families closure, but sometimes in this mad life he'd chosen to live instead of retiring, justice didn't come for everyone if it meant he and Anaisha could get caught for being bent.

He sighed and phoned the twins, George answering, as usual. Colin explained the predicament, and George was in agreement that things would be dealt with swiftly and quietly, but if something super sinister was going on and he felt the UK police had to be informed, then the officer linked to the login and the search on Jamaica would just have to get in the shit. Colin would keep that to himself for now. There was no point in informing Anaisha and her getting upset. That could come later.

"Do you reckon it's people trafficking?" George asked.

"Sounds like it, although I'd say the women are still in the UK, wouldn't you? The hassle of taking them back to Jamaica, or sending them abroad elsewhere, plus that would leave a trail..."

"Fucking hell, I don't want to have to tell Maria any of this."

"Then don't. Keep it to yourself until you know for definite."

"I don't like the idea of leaving all those other families in limbo. Those other women could have been taken by the same people who took Freya—and I'm convinced that's the case now. Those men in the Jaguar..."

"The Jag plates belong to a Vauxhall Corsa by the way."

"Not a surprise. Right, I'll regroup with Greg and get back to you if you're needed."

Colin drove to Janine's. He parked and quietly tapped on her front door, thinking immediately afterwards that he should have messaged her instead. Now he was worried he'd woken Rosie up. Janine answered in a pair of pink pyjamas and flip-flops, looked him up and down, shook her head, and went into the kitchen. Colin followed, taking the Pepsi Max he was supposed to drink on the journey out of his pocket.

"No tea or coffee for me, thanks, and it's not up for debate, not tonight." Lately, he usually let her bully him into drinking tea because every request came from a place of love, she cared enough about him to worry about his health, but he really wasn't in the mood. He sat at a table covered in toys and kid paraphernalia, bending to pick up the basket on the floor so he could help by tidying everything into it. "And I suppose that once-over you gave me was to say I look like a bag of dicks. I know, I'm trying to remember to take care of myself, but it's difficult when I had so many years of someone else doing it for me."

He hadn't said it to gain sympathy, just as a fact. When you spent your whole married life letting someone else cook your food, do you washing, and generally make sure you were okay, it freed you up to think of other things instead. It was taking him some time to remember that he had to do them himself now.

"I gave you a filthy look because there's jam or whatever the hell it might be on your forehead with a few crumbs stuck to it." She turned to the kettle as though what she'd said was the most normal thing ever, and maybe it was now she had Rosie.

Was he that bad? Had he let himself go that much? Granted, he wasn't particularly hot on making sure his appearance was immaculate, some would say he was a scruffy sod, but jam and crumbs?

He pause in packing away the toys and reached up to get rid of it, his fingers encountering a sticky blob. He took one of the wet wipes from the packet on the table and sorted himself out while she made herself a coffee.

"So what job are you on at the moment then?" she asked, taking out a packet of custard creams, probably kept in the cupboard for George.

"At work there's the murder of two old ladies, sisters. Robbery, someone tying them up, beating them, that sort of thing. Nigel thinks it's the nephew, but he has a solid alibi. As for extracurricular activities, a woman called Freya Duncan has been reported missing by her mother. The police basically packed her off, so she turned to the twins." He popped the tab on his cola and went on to tell her what he knew so far.

Janine had drunk her coffee by the time he'd finished. "Bloody Nora, I can see why George would want to help the other families. Eight more women…that's a lot of ripples, aka affected people. But listen, this is the part of the job that I hated, keeping information quiet. The copper in me knew it needed to come out and it would help so many people, but you have to think about yourself, just like Anaisha has to think about *her*self. There's only so much help you can give the twins without dropping yourselves in the crapper, so get over the guilt, because there will be other cases, other guilt trips, it's just par for the course when you work for them."

He nodded. "Mason might come up with something, a lead the twins can use, especially if the women are still alive and being held in the UK. Maybe they'll be returned to their families anonymously."

"That's the ideal solution, but again, you need to get over the guilt if that isn't what happens. You can only do so much before you have to move on. What if it isn't trafficking? What if they're being killed for whatever reason?"

If Colin thought about it all too much then he'd get depressed. He'd been down that spiral when his wife had died and didn't want to go there again. He'd promised himself he'd be happy and live the life she didn't get the chance to finish, and instead of being angry or sad whenever he thought of her, he'd taught himself to smile and be grateful she'd existed in his world at all.

He changed the subject, asking about Rosie.

Best he didn't dwell on Freya and where she might be.

Chapter Twelve

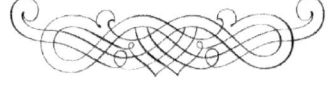

Big B was still at the park. He didn't usually dwell on depressive thoughts, but for some reason he couldn't shake the ones that currently swirled inside his head. It was those imaginings of Sharina being one of the cargo that had done it, and thoughts of how their mother would be devastated if something ever happened to her daughter. Also how she'd be distraught to know that her son played a part in taking women away from their families, all to make some dollars—dollars he couldn't even be seen spending because questions would be asked as to why he was splashing out. There was no flashy car or designer clothes. After all, the small wage he supposedly got from Cheap Fred would barely stretch anywhere, hence why he still lived in the family home.

He was lucky that Fred had agreed to say he worked for him. So long as Big B sent customers Fred's way, then it was cool.

I'm juggling too many balls. I don't want this life anymore. I just want things to be simple.

Some people lived the dream of getting up in the morning with nothing on their to-do list. No phone calls to deal with, no messages or emails to respond to, just a stretch of hours ahead that could be filled doing whatever they wanted. Reading, watching television, going out for a meal, so many things he didn't get to do because he was at the beck and call of the gang.

There was no getting out of it, though, not if he wanted to live.

He got up from the grass and went to sit on a swing, his joints long gone, his mellow mood turning melancholy. Tears burned. Fuck, he'd smoked too much, but it was too late to change it, and any regrets he had would now play out for the rest of the evening, maybe well into the night if he didn't manage to fall asleep.

Did he have the guts to get out, to go back home but live on another part of the island as an anonymous resident? He'd saved enough money that he could live comfortably for a long time if he was careful, but that would mean breaking contact with his mother and sister, keeping well out of their way. He could live in Kingston, they never went there, so there wouldn't be any risk of bumping into them or having to explain why he'd disappeared and to see the disappointment in his mum's eyes when he told her his reason for hiding out.

Then he remembered the gang's promise, that if he ever ran out on them or ratted them out, they'd go after his mother and sister.

"I took the wrong path," he whispered to his mother—pointless because there was no way she'd hear it, but would she feel it? As a mother, would she sense his distress from all those miles away?

She never questioned how he could afford the flights to the UK and why he went there. Was she stupid enough to think that he earned a lot with Fred, or, Jesus Christ, did she know damn well what he did for a living but had chosen to keep her mouth shut?

He got off the swing and began his walk back to the flat, his eyes stinging, his heart wanting what he couldn't have—freedom. And that brought the cargo to mind and how she probably hoped for freedom, too, and if it wasn't for the gang agreeing to choose her, she'd have had it.

Chapter Thirteen

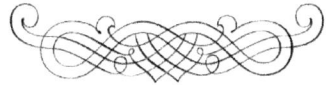

Her holiday had come to an end. When the coach slowed at the junction by the guard hut on the way to the airport, Freya had immediately looked to the right to see if Cool Raffia stood against the lamppost. He hadn't been there, and she'd sagged with relief. Although what had she expected? For the driver to stop and let him on so he could rob the passengers?

She thought, then, about the journey in and how moody the driver had been until he'd stopped to pick up his friend who went by the name of Popcorn. The rep had stayed at the airport after she'd given everyone the information required, so she likely had no idea this man had boarded the bus.

Popcorn had tried to sell weed to the lads in the seats behind Freya, but they'd all declined. Then the driver had announced a stop halfway along, and he'd parked outside a two-storey shack made of wood that had a wonky CAFÉ/BAR *sign on the front in yellow with black font. One of the lads had got off to buy some drinks and had returned to complain about how many dollars it had cost him to get six stubby bottles of Corona. Was it a stretch to think that the driver split any profits for drug selling with Popcorn, and maybe he'd also get commission for bringing naïve tourists to the café. Did that beer cost as much for the locals? She doubted it.*

The journey to the airport had been bittersweet — she wanted to stay and she wanted to go home. She'd loved the majority of her time away but not the reason for it. She'd proved to herself that she could do something on her own, though, and such a big thing, too, taking a long-haul flight. And she'd successfully swept a lot of bitter emotions under the carpet regarding James and Theresa, coming to the conclusion that she and James were clearly not meant to be together, and if she got home and found out he'd set up home with Theresa now, then there was no point moping about it. Moping wouldn't change the outcome, it wouldn't bring James back, and anyway, Freya didn't want to be with someone who could so easily being distracted by another woman.

The problem she had now was that James had seemed so sincere and honest throughout their relationship that she was going to find it difficult to trust another man again if he acted the same way. She'd always be waiting for the other shoe to drop. He'd messaged this morning to thank her for giving him space to move out of her flat, and if he'd accidentally left anything behind, he'd appreciate her letting him know so he could collect it. She wasn't the sort to put things in the bin, she wasn't vindictive enough, therefore she also wasn't the type to get hold of Theresa's husband and tell him what had been going on, even though Lottie had encouraged her to do it. Maybe morally she had a duty to inform him, so he wasn't being duped any longer either, but honestly, it was down to his wife to come clean. Why should Freya bear the brunt of any anger that was sure to come her way for being the messenger? And how could she live with herself for being the one to open that particular can of worms if it meant Theresa's child went through hell with his parents splitting up acrimoniously?

The airport had been an eye-opener, nothing like the ones at home, the queuing process long and arduous and so very hot. The conveyer belt that took the cases after they'd been weighed had broken, and it seemed none of the airline reps gave a fiddler's fuck at the chaos it created. There had still been plenty of time before boarding, though, and Freya had been able to join yet another long queue in the food area to get herself a Wendy's burger.

Finally on the plane, there had been another delay of an hour due to the conveyor belt issue. It had meant some of the cases hadn't made it onto the plane yet, so they had to wait until they'd been loaded. With takeoff out of the way and the first round of drinks offered by the cabin crew, she watched a film with Mr Bean in it, then had a nap. Soon the first meal arrived, a roast chicken dinner only enough to fill a child's belly, and then she browsed to find another film. She chose Wonka, *despite having watched it three times before, and towards the end found herself drifting off.*

She woke to a black screen on the seat in front and on the majority of the others in the vicinity. The lights above had dimmed, and a lot of people were asleep. She dozed on and off for the next hour, waking with a start because she sensed someone was staring at her. She had an aisle seat, so it was likely there might be a queue for the toilet, but she opened her eyes to find a Jamaican man with a scar in his eyebrow studying her. She frowned, hoping he got the gist that she didn't like what he was doing. He sucked his teeth at her as if she'd done something to offend him, then walked towards the back of the plane. Freya looked at the other two passengers beside her to see if they'd noticed the exchange, but they were both asleep. The three people in the middle aisle hadn't seen anything either — all of them had their eyes closed.

She kept hers open until the man came back. He paused beside her seat again and glanced at her before moving on. She poked her head out into the aisle to see where he sat, but he went past the open dividing curtain and into the other section on the other side of the wings.

She shrugged it off. Maybe her foot had been sticking out while she'd been asleep and that's what he'd been annoyed about. There was nothing she could do about it anyway, what was done was done, so she unrolled the little blanket the airline had provided and tucked it around her, settling down again for another nap.

She woke to the smell of food and the lights getting gradually brighter as though they mimicked the sun rising. Weirdly, it had the desired effect because Freya felt quite alert despite having fractured sleep throughout the flight. She folded the blanket and popped it on her lap, then brought the table in front down, ready for her breakfast.

It was good—yoghurt, a muffin, and a multigrain bar along with slightly frozen orange juice, a roll and butter, and a cup of tea or coffee. Afterwards she had to move out of the way so the other two passengers could use the toilet, then she went herself, choosing to go to the one at the back so she didn't have to go past that strange man.

An hour or so later, the pilot announced that they were flying towards Cornwall and would be over the Isle of Wight shortly. Both the flight to Jamaica and this one had gone surprisingly quickly, much faster than she'd imagined, and in no time the wheels hit the runway and everyone clapped. Relieved to be on solid ground, Freya popped her earphones in her bumbag, took her phone off flight mode, and checked for any messages that had come in.

JAMES: I LEFT THE KEYS ON THE SIDE IN THE KITCHEN.

She didn't know why he'd felt the need to say that when she'd have seen them for herself when she got home anyway. Had he used it as an excuse to contact her? Had he been telling her the truth regarding his chats with Theresa, that in his eyes they were innocent even though they looked anything but at times? The thing was, just chatting to Theresa the way he had was enough for Freya to lose faith in him, not to mention trust, and in her eyes there had been no point in continuing their relationship if she knew damn well she'd always be suspicious of him in the future.

She hadn't told him she was going on holiday, just that she wouldn't be in when he collected his things, although if he snooped around it wouldn't take a rocket scientist to know that her suitcase was missing. Mum and Lottie wouldn't pass on the fact she'd spent the last two weeks in Jamaica, especially because she'd asked them not to, and a part of her hoped that he saw her when she got back, saw her tan so he'd know she'd had the guts to do something he'd never thought she could. Be by herself. Manage things all on her own.

When she thought about it, he was condescending in that regard. He'd always wanted to do everything for her, and in the end it had looked like she was incapable of doing anything for herself. Maybe that's why she'd chosen to go on holiday on her own, to prove she was capable.

Freya collected her hand luggage from the overhead compartment and followed everyone else off into the tunnel. She went through passport control and into the baggage area, wondering if her case was still in Jamaica because of the snafu at the airport in Montego Bay. No, there it was, her bright-yellow luggage on the carousel. She rushed forward to get it, tapping elbows with someone beside her.

"Sorry," she said as she hauled her case off and onto the floor, then turned to smile at the person to show that she hadn't jabbed them on purpose.

It was the weird man from the plane.

"Oh," she blurted at the same time her heart rate accelerated.

He glared at her, tutted, then switched his attention to the carousel. He reached out for a small black case, so she hurried away with hers, desperate to rush through NOTHING TO DECLARE *and get the hell out of the airport.*

On her way to the door, a big black man walked past and gave her a look as if to apologise for the one with the scar. Why would he do that, though? Had they travelled together? And shit, wasn't he the man who'd warned her to be careful when she got home? The one from the beach who'd said she'd had the tour? She glanced around to double-check, but he'd already gone.

She rushed outside to see if she could catch up with him, but he wasn't there. The cooler UK air was expected and something she'd longed for at times while she'd been away, but now that she stood staring at the bus stops for the transport from the terminals to the car park offices where she'd pick up her car keys, she suddenly wanted to be back where it was hot. Thankful she'd thought to pop her cardigan in her hand luggage, she took it out and put it on and then boarded one of the buses. She stowed her case then sat at the back, her nerves on fire when she spotted the scarred man getting on and sitting by the exit. Then the big man got on, but he didn't sit beside him, nor did he look at her.

She panicked for the whole journey, but once the bus stopped and Scar got off along with everyone else, she lost sight of him—and the big man. They hadn't gone into the office, she knew that much, so maybe there was another bus that would take them to wherever they were going.

She had to force herself to believe they hadn't followed her from Jamaica, that it was just a coincidence.

RAFFIA

It didn't take long to sign the form to get her car back, then she was getting in it and heading towards her flat. It would be odd to see it without James' things there, but it was something she was going to have to get used to.

It was time to dive into single life again.

Chapter Fourteen

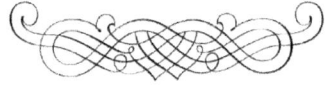

Another day dawned without the sound of the waves. Big B lay in bed, a huge wedge of resentment in his chest regarding the decisions he'd made. Before sleep last night, he'd chastised himself for making wrong calls, for not seeing his recruitment for what it was and how he'd been manipulated along the way.

RAFFIA

At the very beginning, when he'd been asked to sit in the van to make up the numbers, he hadn't felt threatened or forced into it. The other members had been friendly, still were, and he hadn't sensed any type of worry that what he was doing was wrong. If only he hadn't taken the dollars handed to him that day, but his maturity level had been so much lower. He'd had to grow up a lot since those early days, accepting the stark realisation that what he was doing was so much more than taking a bit of money from tourists. And, God, how insidiously it had all happened — he'd being promoted to each new level without fanfare which had further convinced him he wasn't doing anything wrong. Or maybe he'd been convincing himself it wasn't so he didn't have to feel guilty.

Today really wasn't the day he ought to be ripping himself a new arsehole. The beginning of the next step had arrived — the hawk that had flown the nest must have landed by now. Big B still had no idea which bird had flown from Jamaica to help him with the cargo. The one who'd been with him on the flight to England had already gone back.

His phone bleated, and he read the message.

Digby Dog: Go to the usual meeting spot and wait.

He let out an excess of breath, collected his cigarettes and lighter, and left the flat. Floppy Tits was just coming out of her flat as he went past. He wasn't in the mood to get an earful off her, but she smiled, and he remembered something his mum had once said: "You never know what someone's going through behind their smile."

You never know what they're going through behind a scowl either.

"Wagwan," he said.

"Morning. Off somewhere nice?"

"Just to meet a friend. You?"

"Food shopping." She took a breath, as if gearing herself up, then said, "Thanks for not…you know, not having a go at me when I spoke to you last night."

"S'all right."

"You look like you've got the weight of the world on your shoulders."

"I've got a weight, yeah. Nothing that can be done about it, though."

"Something can always be done."

That was true enough, but the options open to him were extremely limited, and whichever one he took, he may well lose his life.

"I've got time for a coffee if you need to talk," she said.

That was a complete change from her attitude last night, but maybe she'd had an epiphany like him, a moment when she'd tried to fall asleep and she'd wished things were different—that *she* was different. She could help herself a lot by not moaning for a start.

He checked the time on his phone. "I can't let my friend down." But then he remembered the meet-up time, and if he ran from wherever they had coffee with fifteen minutes to spare, he'd get there. "Fuck, okay."

She went along the walkway first, and he followed her down the piss-stinking stairs and out onto the path. The sun blazed, and sweat popped out on his eyebrows. Around the corner the café loomed like a warning for him not to go inside—he had a bad feeling, but if he kept his wits about him and a rein on his words, he'd be all right.

"Bloody hot, isn't it?" she asked.

"Much hotter where I'm from. This is nothing."

"Where are you from?"

"Jamaica."

"Are you here on holiday?"

"Yeah."

He was saved from further probing; she pushed into the café and strode to the top corner by the till, flumping down and letting out a sigh. The air-conditioning was an instant relief, and he sat opposite her, letting her order a pot of tea each and a few slices of toast.

"Assuming that's what you want," she said.

He took a tenner out of his wallet and put it on the table. At her frown, he said, "You mentioned you had it tough. Last night."

"Oh yeah. Thanks." When the server walked off, Floppy Tits leaned back and folded her arms. "So what's up with you, then?"

"It's not something I can talk about—not just in public but with anyone."

"So you're into dodgy shit, are you?"

"You could say that."

"And?"

"I want to get out."

"So get out."

"It's not that easy."

"Oh."

"It's gang related."

"Ouch. Erm, are you doing gang-related shit while here on holiday?"

"Um, yeah?"

"Then watch your back, okay?"

His heart skipped a beat. "What do you mean?"

"Have you heard about London leaders?"

He shook his head.

She launched into an explanation, and he wondered why the fuck no one had mentioned anything about this.

"Shit," he said.

"There are spies everywhere, just so you know."

He eyed her. "Are you one of them?"

She laughed, "If I was, I wouldn't be skint, would I. You get paid for being a grass."

"Will you grass on me?"

"Nah."

"Why not?"

She shrugged. "I sense we're kindred spirits. Both down on our luck—or down on something anyway. And you want to get out of whatever it is you're in, so you can't be all that bad." She stopped talking while the server put their tea and toast down. "The twins will probably help you."

From what she'd told him about men called The Brothers, he didn't hold out much hope. They wanted their Estate nice and tidy and were in the process of cleaning it up. They were more likely to get rid of him as a stain on their patch. Someone who did bad things and should be 'disappeared'.

"They're not going to help me, not after what I've done."

She poured tea, and he checked the time. He'd have to go soon. A quick butter of toast with a thin spread of jam, and they sat quietly, Floppy Tits on her phone playing some game or other.

"What's your name?" he asked.

She looked up from her screen. "Why, are you going to get your friends to sort me out, shut me up in case I tell the twins something? Like the fact you're staying next door to me? Listen, I don't need the hassle, and to be honest, what I don't know won't hurt me, so if you don't blab to me about what you get up to, there's nothing I need to keep quiet, is there?"

He nodded and finished his slice of toast. He drank half of his tea, then stood. "I have to go."

"You know where I am if you fancy a chat later."

He nodded. "Thanks for breakfast."

He walked out, the weight of the world she'd mentioned lifting slightly. The odd premonition he'd had when approaching the café no longer existed. Something told him he could trust Floppy Tits.

She never told me her name.

Instead of jogging like he'd planned, he hopped on a bus that drew in at just the right moment. Sitting out of the way at the back, he stared at the passing streets, the people, betting they didn't have a massive problem like he did.

He got off and walked to the meeting spot, taking the route by memory. He'd only done it twice before in person but had travelled virtually via Google Maps several times. A dart left down an alley, and he came out the other end behind a row of shops, delivery bays hidden by high gates. The hawk stepped out from the Tesco Express yard, and Big B's heart sank.

What the fuck's he *doing here?*

Chapter Fifteen

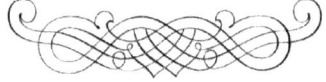

Fish and Chips, aka Noel and Joel, twins otherwise known as the Unidenticals, sat in a stolen Range Rover waiting for the Jamaicans to show up. The one who'd introduced himself as Big B had messaged to say his friend had arrived and it wouldn't be long before the cargo would be moved to another location. They wanted to chat about the logistics in person rather than leave too much of a trail on their phones. Some messaging was inevitable, as were phone calls, but Noel wasn't a fan of evidence being left behind either, and when their part in this job was over, he'd ditch the burner they'd been using and pretend none of this had ever happened.

He hadn't much liked Big B or the man he'd brought with him, some scarred bastard with an attitude, but their mate from the Jamaican community had asked Noel and Joel to do him a favour—for ten grand—and neither twin had a mind to say no.

"He said he's bringing someone else this time." Noel watched the road ahead for signs of the men.

Nothing.

"I don't like it when they change the rules halfway through," Joel said.

"Me neither."

From the start, they'd been assured the contacts would be Big B and Mr Attitude. As far as Noel was concerned, the less chess pieces involved in the game the better, but this outfit seemed to know what they were doing, and if their contact was to be believed, this little project had been carried out successfully in the UK before.

"Why do you need us, then?" he'd asked Rudy Dude during their first meeting—the scarred fella.

"Best for us not to keep using the same people. One piece of cargo per contact."

It made sense, and if Noel and Joel didn't get too involved, it was less for them to worry about afterwards. They could walk away, richer, and not think about it again. Not that Noel wanted to think about that poor cow in Puggy's spare room, but ten grand was ten grand, and besides, it only looked like she'd had a couple of clips around the face. It wasn't like she'd gone ten rounds in the ring.

He was ashamed of himself for thinking that way. He really ought to take a long, hard look at himself. Then there was Puggy, someone Noel had vowed not to use anymore on account of him being a bit touched in the head. And 'touched in the head' wasn't a term he ought to be using, but he didn't know what was up with Puggy, just that he wasn't all there.

"Here they come." Joel pointed out of the windscreen. "What the fuck's up with *that* fella?"

Noel stared at the man with Big B. He limped—was his leg bent inwards at one of the knees?—and it looked like he didn't own a single tooth. His tight-fitting jeans emphasised his obvious affliction, but he had a mean-arse look on his sour face that suggested Noel and Joel ought to be careful.

"Is this a joke?" Joel whispered.

"I don't think so somehow."

Both Jamaicans reached the bonnet then split ways, Big B getting in the back behind Joel, the other geezer sitting behind Noel.

"All right?" Noel asked.

"Wagwan," Big B said. "How's the cargo?"

"To be honest, we haven't been to see her. Considering we only ever visit there with balaclavas on, and because you said the less attention we draw to the flat, the better..." *In other words, why the fuck would we go and see the cargo when you basically told us not to? Dickhead.*

"Good. I was just checking. Any updates from that Piggy man?"

"Puggy not Piggy. No, which is good, it means he has things under control."

"Where is the flat?" the other man asked.

"This is Cool Raffia," Big B butted in. "If he's asking for the location, then it means he's been asked by those higher up where it is. There will be a reason."

Why hadn't Big B told him where the cargo was? He'd dropped her off there the other night with the scarred fucker, for God's sake. Maybe in their gang it wasn't his place to offer information. Or maybe this Cool Raffia geezer was the type to ask for it so it looked like he'd gleaned information he wasn't supposed to have and it made him feel important.

"Our man is vulnerable," Noel said. "We told you that. He doesn't like strangers coming to his door."

"No one will touch your man," Mr Cool said.

Joel recited the address on a sigh of annoyance. "But don't go there and upset him. He's temperamental."

"A wide boy?" Mr Cool asked.

"No, he gets worried easily. It's a big enough thing for him to look after the cargo, so any extra on top…any visits from you… Do you get what I'm saying? He's a good lad, and I don't want him fretting."

Big B looked at Mr Cool and nodded. "We won't upset him." He leaned forward between the front seats. "We'll meet you at the flat at two a.m. to remove the cargo."

"Fine. And you'll bring the other half of our payment?"

"Of course." Big B got out of the car.

Mr Cool, who didn't look cool at all, bared his gums in what must amount to a smile. "You keep your mouth shut when we part ways tonight, yeah, man?"

"Yep," Noel said. "We're not green, we know how this shit works."

Mr Cool frowned. "Why are you hiding your faces?"

"Isn't it obvious? Barely anyone knows what we look like, and if they don't know, they can't pass on a description—all in your favour if this shit blows up."

"Why would it blow up?"

"I was speaking hypothetically."

"Right."

The man got out and hobbled off up the road to where Big B waited a few cars down.

"What an absolutely irritating cunt," Noel said.

Chapter Sixteen

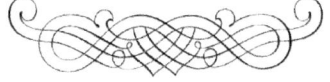

Puggy woke to the sound of thuds on the wall. They weren't overly loud, just Income letting him know that the bucket was full, most likely, and the smell could no longer be tolerated. It must be nasty to always smell that, especially if she was in the cupboard with the bucket. For there to be thuds, it meant he must have overslept. Mind you, he'd been up late last night. He couldn't stop thinking about how nice it was to meet the people at the dance class, and Sarah had messaged him, too.

He rolled over, his legs sticking together from sweat, and glanced at the clock on the bedside cabinet. It was after ten o'clock. He'd usually sorted breakfast by now. He was so tempted to put his head under the quilt like he would have months ago, back when he was his old slobby self and lived in a hovel. Even though it was so stuffy in his room, he could just go back to sleep so he could forget his job for the day, but then he remembered Fish and Chips were due round with his money later, and that gave him the incentive to get up.

He opened the thick curtains, bright sunlight slapping him in the face. He leaned his palms on the sill, snatching them back when his skin got too hot, then opened the window to let some air in. He managed to keep it open for forty-two seconds, but then the banging started again so he had to shut it.

He made his bed so he didn't forget to do it later. Shawnee, the woman who'd dropped drugs round for his last job, said that making your bed first thing, even if it meant not airing it, set your mind up to accept that the first task of the day had been done, which in turn would make you want to get on with the next one, and so on, until your day was complete. It actually worked, so he did what she'd told him to do regarding the bathroom, too.

He wished he could see Shawnee again so he could tell her how well her advice worked. He did everything she'd told him to, every day, and that was why he'd been able to keep the flat so clean and tidy, not to mention himself. But she never came round anymore. A shame, that.

He dried himself off, slipping on his dressing gown, and squirted bleach down the toilet, although it might get dirty again soon when he emptied the bucket. Bugger. In his room, he got dressed and took the washing out of the hamper, taking it straight to the washing machine and doing a load along with his towel. It was hot enough to hang the laundry out later, something he'd never done before because he'd just shoved it on a drying cycle in the machine, but Shawnee was so right, it saved him a lot on his electric meter. Once his load was done, he'd ask Income for her clothes. They were probably smelly by now, and he had an old tracksuit and some underpants she could put on in the meantime.

He collected the mail from the mat, nodding to himself at the envelope the twins had popped through after dark. He stuffed the fifty quid inside a packet of Shredded Wheat—it'd be safe in there. He made bacon sandwiches for breakfast, leaving his plate on the worktop under some clingfilm. There were a lot of flies this summer. That was another reason he was glad to keep on top of the housework. Last year, a fly had laid some eggs on a loaf of bread he'd left open, and when he'd gone to make some toast, maggots had been everywhere.

Cup of tea and the other plate of food on a tray, Puggy took them into the spare room, recoiling at the stench mixed with the oppressive heat. He'd like to open the window but couldn't trust that Income would keep quiet. This bedroom faced the back, but there was an alley down the side by his garden that anyone could go down. They might hear the noise. He placed the breakfast on the floor and untied her wrists from the bedpost.

"You should go and sit in the cupboard now."

Income did that, hopping along as her ankles were tied, and Puggy put the rope in his pocket.

Best to be safe and not leave it behind, and he'd need it again later anyway. He kept a wary eye on Income while he bent to pick up the breakfast, taking it over and placing it on the floor near the cupboard. A quick flick of his wrist and he'd snatched the socks out of her mouth, hoping she didn't take it as an invitation for a chat. Puggy picked up the shit-and-piss bucket and left her to it, praying today wasn't the day she chose to scream.

He poured the contents of the bucket down the toilet, cleaned the bucket, then scrubbed the toilet again. He was going to need some more bleach soon. He returned the bucket to the cupboard. Income had swivelled round so her legs stuck out, which prevented him from shutting the door. That was okay, there wasn't much in here that he could be hurt with if she got up and went for him. There was just the bed, a pillow, a quilt, and the bucket.

"I've just cleaned the bathroom, but you can have a shower if you want. Your bum must be smelly." He felt bad, but there was no way he was going to wipe it for her whenever the bucket was used for a number two. "I'll have to sit on the toilet and watch you like last time, though." He hadn't watched *properly*, he wasn't a pervert, he'd just kept his sights to the side of her naked body, enough that he could see what was going on and anticipate any attack. Fish had warned him about that. "I'll wash your clothes, too. I'll be back in half an hour."

He ate his breakfast standing at the kitchen window. No lads out there this morning, they'd have all gone to school, but a woman sat on a blanket on the grass, her face turned to the sky. Sunlight reflected off the windows on the houses opposite, and the road shimmered with heat; he reckoned the tarmac might get spongy today.

He finished his sandwich, drank his tea, and hung the washing out, chuffed to bits to be so productive, even if he was behind from oversleeping. It really was hot already, and the flat would be an oven if he wasn't careful. Sometimes he forgot things, like switching on his fans. Maybe he could put one in the hallway, pointed so the cool air filtered in underneath the spare room door. Or, he could take it into the room and place it in the far corner, tying Income to the bed so he couldn't be hit with the fan the next time he went in.

It hurt his brain having to be forward-thinking, working out the steps ahead before he did them.

He closed the door to the garden and locked it, then got on with the business of Income having a shower. She promised not to hurt him if he untied her ankles and took the handcuffs off, and he believed her. He removed them so she could get undressed, then he held her wrist and took her to the bathroom.

Like the last time, even though he'd been on his guard, Puggy found he didn't have to worry about anything. Income got into the bath without any hassle, washed all over underneath the spray of water, and got out to allow him to hand over a towel. She dried herself, although her hair remained dripping wet. Back in the spare room, he removed the towel, took the rope from his pocket, and tied Income to the bedpost. He collected new socks and stuffed them in her mouth, then went off to find one of his five fans.

"I know I'm not supposed to be letting you have a shower and stuff, and I'll get in trouble if they know I've let you have a fan, but it's hot, isn't it, and you hear about dogs and kids suffocating in cars when the windows aren't open, and I don't want that to happen to you. I'd be in trouble with the police. They might say I'd murdered you."

The thought of that shit the life out of him, so he grabbed the towel and ran from the room, twisting the key in the lock and popping it in his pocket. He collected the dirty clothes from the bathroom and put them in the washing machine with the towel, then remembered he hadn't handed over the tracksuit and underpants, but he didn't want to go back into that bedroom and see…see the fear in those eyes.

To stop himself from spiralling into manic thoughts, he cleaned the bathroom again, remembering that he'd left the bucket in the cupboard, too far away, so if Income wanted a poo or wee she'd have to do it on the bed.

A loud knock had him clutching the bleach bottle in front of the toilet, his heart whomping so hard he felt sick. It was a different kind of knock to the thuds that Income made, and he waited for the cargo to make a racket in a bid for help, despite him explaining that if she was too noisy there'd be trouble. But Income was being good, she must realise that the knock had been made by someone important—or was it because he'd pushed the socks far back into her mouth so any shouts were muffled?

He tucked the bleach away behind the toilet and quickly washed his hands. Shawnee had said it was important to do that after cleaning the bathroom because there were so many germs around. He dried them on his tracksuit bottoms and walked down the hallway, frowning at the shapes behind the mottled glass. They weren't wide or tall enough for the twins. The same went for Fish and Chips. There weren't the right curves for Miss Daulton either. So who had come?

Nervous, he looked through the spyhole.

"Open up. Fish told us where to come," a man said.

Puggy studied the distorted face on the other side of the door. The black man with short hair didn't have many teeth, and he stood a little lopsided beside another man.

He was here the other night when they brought Income.

"I'm not allowed to let anyone in," Puggy said loudly.

The letterbox flapped open, startling him. He bent over to look through the gap.

A pair of eyes stared back at him.

"Wagwan."

Puggy didn't know what that meant and reversed into the kitchen, grabbing his phone. The men moved to stand in front of the window and gawped in at him, so he turned his back and checked whether Fish and Chips had sent any messages. They hadn't.

What am I supposed to do?

He darted back round to pull the blind cord, blocking the men out. A knock came on the window, and Puggy all but jumped a mile. He whimpered, panicking, and then remembered one of the rules: *If someone is at the door and they shouldn't be, go into the spare room and lock yourself in. Contact us, then wait.*

Puggy hurried down the hallway, fumbling with the key in the lock, so conscious of the knocking at the front door and the eyes appearing in the letterbox slit again. He threw himself into the spare room, locking it, turning to find Income watching him warily. He quickly brought up the number he had for Fish and Chips and pressed the icon to connect the call.

"What's up?" Fish asked.

"Men are here," Puggy said. "One of them is from the other night."

"Fuck's sake, I knew you shouldn't have told him where she is."

"I didn't," Puggy said.

"I wasn't talking to you, I was talking to Chips."

"But Big B knew anyway," Chips said.

"What do they look like?" Fish asked.

Panic built. This conversation was confusing.

"Did you say that to me?" Puggy asked.

"*Yes!*"

Puggy described them.

"Jesus. Okay, stay put. We'll be over in a minute."

Puggy sank to the floor in front of the door, waiting for his phone screen to go blank. Then he thought about Income having no clothes on and how embarrassing that would be if the men came in with Fish and Chips. He rushed out and into his bedroom, fetching the tracksuit and underpants.

In the spare room, tightly locked away, he stared at Income. He'd forgotten to tie her ankles. Oh God. He couldn't cope with the hassle of getting her dressed so draped the clothes over her, then, despite it being so muggy, pulled the quilt over. He wished he'd never agreed to do this babysitting, but he was in it up to his neck now, and Fish wouldn't let him back out. They wanted his spare room, and that was the end of it.

Puggy wanted to cry.

Chapter Seventeen

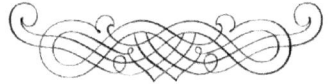

The phone call from Puggy hadn't been expected—but maybe it should have been. There was something about Mr Not Cool that had rubbed Noel up the wrong way. And of *course* the Jamaicans had gone to the fucking flat despite saying they wouldn't. Why, though?

"I bet they've gone there to collect the woman now so they can fuck off with the rest of our money," Noel said as they drove towards Puggy's place. "Bastards."

"Big B didn't strike me as the type to fuck us over, though."

"Looks and mannerisms can be deceptive. *We* didn't strike me as people who'd get involved with this sort of shit after that business with Tommy Coda and Leanora, but here we are."

"Don't start yapping on about that French woman again. Try to just think about the money. No, we don't particularly need it, but it's nice to have it for doing fuck all. Let's be honest, it's Puggy doing all the work, feeding her and whatever."

Joel parked round the back of the block of flats, and without needing to discuss it, they jogged down the alley that spanned the back of the flats then down another beside Puggy's garden. At the front of the building, Noel poked one eye round. Big B and Mr Not Cool stood by Puggy's front door, Cool staring through the letterbox. Noel reared back round the corner and indicated for Joel to follow him. They climbed over the gate.

"What's going on?" Joel whispered.

"Big B and that gammy-legged fucker are at the front door."

"Shit. What do you want to do now?"

"I'm going to have to warn Puggy, but there's a part of me that wants to get hold of our UK Jamaican contact who put this job our way in the first place."

"And say what?"

"To shove this up his fucking arse. It's more hassle than it's worth."

"Bog off! The amount we're getting paid is worth it."

They stood by the back door, and Noel sent Puggy a message: WE'RE IN YOUR GARDEN. LOOK OUT OF THE WINDOW.

A curtain moved aside just a tad, and one of Puggy's eyes appeared. He vanished, the curtain swinging back into place, then a message blipped on Noel's phone.

PUGGY: WHAT ARE WE GOING TO DO?

NOEL: ME AND CHIPS WILL GO ROUND THE FRONT TO TALK TO THEM, MAKE THEM GO AWAY, THEN I'LL MESSAGE YOU.

PUGGY: [THUMBS-UP EMOJI]

Noel launched himself over the gate first, landing hard and making a loud thud.

"Wait," he whispered to his twin and winced, staring towards the front of the building, his heart hammering while he waited for the Jamaicans to poke their heads around and spot him there. Ten heartbeats, twenty, and he reckoned it would be all right. "You're good to go."

Joel vaulted over, and they walked to the front, presenting themselves to the men still at the door. Big B jumped upon seeing them, gesturing to a bent-over Mr Not Cool as if to tell them it was all his fault that they were there.

"I asked you not to bother our man." Noel stepped forward and gripped the back of Cool's shirt.

"What the fuck? Get *off* me!"

Noel pulled him over to the grass, giving him a shove then letting him go. Cool landed on his hands and knees, springing up with surprising agility, considering his knee, and squared up to Noel, his chest puffed up.

Noel couldn't help himself. He laughed. "Seriously? You seriously think I should be afraid of you?" He gestured to the size of himself. "Fuck right off."

Cool backed off a few steps, his hands raised.

"Let him see the cargo," Big B said. "That's all he wants to do."

Noel narrowed his eyes at Mr Not Cool. "Why, doesn't he trust she's there?"

Big B shook his head. "He trusts no one, especially not you two. It's the covered faces."

"It's how we always work, our mutual contact knows that. Maybe he chose us for that reason—that and we can be trusted to keep the cargo hidden."

Mr Not Cool backed off some more. "I just want to see that it's the *right* target."

"Of *course* it is," Big B hissed at him, seemingly offended. "I sent pictures after we landed."

"I want to see her in the flesh."

Noel looked at Joel who nodded.

Noel sent a message: BRING THE CARGO INTO THE HALLWAY.

PUGGY: OKAY. THEN WHAT?

NOEL: THEN YOU TAKE HER BACK INTO THE BEDROOM AND LOCK YOURSELVES IN.

PUGGY: [THUMBS-UP EMOJI]

"You'll see her in a second," Noel said. "Look through the letterbox."

Mr Not Cool wobbled over to the door and crouched.

Chapter Eighteen

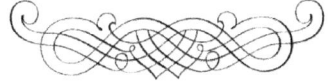

Puggy put his phone in his pocket, never so glad to see Fish and Chips. He usually dreaded it, but not today, not when those other men were here.

"We've got to go out into the hallway," he said and stepped forward to undo the rope tying Income to the bedpost. "I'll wrap the quilt around you so they don't see your private parts." He got on with that, hoping she wouldn't be staying here for too much longer. Yes, he liked the money, but he felt bad for the way he had to treat her. "Come on."

He led her to the door. For whatever reason, she didn't do anything but follow him out into the hallway, meek and mild. If he were in the same shoes, he'd kick up a fuss and try to run away, out of the back door and into the garden, naked or not.

He caught sight of the letterbox being open, those horrible eyes filling the slit.

Income glanced that way.

And screamed a muffled scream.

Chapter Nineteen

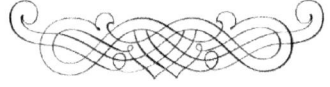

Walking into the flat after it'd been closed up for two weeks was like Jamaica hadn't even happened and she was stepping into her old life again, minus James and all his things. And it felt weird. Even though she'd wanted nothing more than for him to take his stuff away so she could arrive home with it not there, it was odd not to see his shoes by the rack, his

jacket hanging from the hook above, or his keys in the bowl on the slim table by the front door. Instead the latter were on the side in the kitchen, along with a note which basically repeated what he'd said in his text about leaving the keys there. It annoyed her that he seemed to think she was stupid if she needed the information repeated. Maybe it was because she hadn't responded to the text that he'd wondered whether it had even gone through, but no, he'd have seen it had because it would have had READ *at the bottom.*

She had to stop making excuses for him.

And anyway, what did she care what he thought? He hadn't cared about her thoughts when he'd been talking to that woman, so Freya owed him nothing. Once again she told herself off for thinking about him, but it was difficult when this was the home they'd shared and his absence was so glaringly obvious.

She'd spent some time with her mother and Lottie the day after she'd got back, then she had to return to work, so there had been no time to unpack. It was Friday evening now, and she had the massive urge to wind down by herself and be left alone. Going to the Noodle on Tuesday night with Lottie had been fun, but she'd

been bombarded with questions, then there had been the couple of hundred emails she'd had to deal with when she'd gone back to the office, so she felt like she needed a break again already.

She busied herself by taking the dirty washing out of her suitcase and putting a load into the machine. While the drum swished her clothes around, she unpacked the rest, already wishing for another holiday, seeing as the Jamaican one had been tainted. Or maybe she'd just got the travel bug and needed to be away from London and all the memories there. Maybe she ought to move to Liverpool like she'd once thought about. She'd be alone at first but would soon make friends.

By the time she'd finished putting everything away, hanging the first load of washing on one of the three airers in the spare room, and stuffing the second load in the machine, she was hungry. She'd nip around the corner and get a pizza and a bottle of wine, maybe some sweets, then she'd hang the second load up and spend the rest of the evening on the sofa.

Tomorrow she'd visit Mum and Lottie, perhaps finally let them know what had happened to her so they'd understand her reasons for moving away a bit more. Mum had already texted a few times this evening, but Freya hadn't had the energy to answer all of them except for the first, which was to confirm she was going to spend a quiet evening by herself. She had so much on her mind now she just needed an evening to herself with no distractions.

No distractions apart from a lovely pizza and a prosecco.

Chapter Twenty

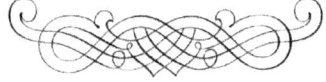

Freya sat on the bed and stared at the poor kid who'd been tasked with looking after her. He'd been good to her so far, and it was obvious he was being used because he was someone easy to manipulate. Was that how she was seen, too? Some stupid woman easily snatched and brought to a flat, the majority of her time spent in a built-in cupboard or roped to the post of a single bed?

"You're scared of them," she said, thankful he hadn't put the socks back in her mouth but now worried he'd remember to do it because she'd spoken.

"I don't like nasty men." He sat on the bed next to her. "One time, these other nasty men came to my door, except they weren't nasty really. I thought they were because that's what Shawnee said, but they were the twins, and they promised to look after me. They said if anything bad happened I was supposed to message them or ring them, but those men out the front… I don't think I'd better open my mouth. They'd hurt me."

At the mention of the twins, hope spread in her chest in the form of a warm surge. But what if that hope had come from her hearing something she wanted to hear? "Do you mean The Brothers?"

"Yeah, but if they find out I've been working for Fish and Chips again…"

He'd mentioned that before, and she assumed they were nicknames. "Who are they?"

"The men in balaclavas."

"Why can't you tell the twins about them?"

"They'll want to know who Fish and Chips are, but Fish and Chips have told me I'm not allowed to tell anyone or they'll come round here and hit me, even though Fish said he didn't want to hit me again. He punched me once and was really sorry afterwards. George and Greg ask me about them every now and again, but I'm too frightened to say anything—I used to sell drugs for Fish and Chips, see. And I don't really know who they are anyway because of the balaclavas. I don't know where they live, and they don't always come here in the same car, so I can't even tell the twins that."

Something wasn't sitting right. "How did you get involved with them? Fish and Chips, I mean."

"They came here one day and asked me if I wanted to earn some pocket money. It was looking after boxes for someone called Andre. Then they asked me if I'd sell baggies that were in the boxes whenever someone knocked on the door. I got good money for it until Shawnee came here and everything went wrong."

She made a mental note to ask who Shawnee was, but a more important subject needed to be discussed. "How did Fish and Chips know to come here?"

He cuffed spit from his bottom lip. "I don't know."

"How come they picked you?"

"I don't *know*."

"What I'm trying to say is, they must know you, and you must know them, for them to have even come here in the first place. They're probably using the face masks so you don't recognise them. They're not just going to pick a random person to sell drugs for some man, are they?"

"I don't know."

Frustrated that she wasn't getting anywhere, or maybe because he didn't see what she was getting at, she asked, "Who's Shawnee?"

"She was lovely. She came here with the boxes sometimes, to drop them off. Had a cup of tea once or twice. And then she stayed here and taught me how to clean the flat, and do the washing, and soak my underpants in the bowl in the kitchen."

Freya held back a shudder at why underpants needed to soak in a bowl. But then she checked herself. Who was she to be judgemental, considering she had to shit in a bucket and had no way to wipe herself unless he took her to the toilet. That didn't happen enough, but she'd got used to the smell.

"It sounds as if she liked helping you," she said.

"Yeah, but The Brothers explained that she wasn't nice really, that she'd killed Andre and stole his life. I don't know how you steal someone's life, but that's what she did. I have no idea where she is anymore. They took her away."

Freya had heard about what the leaders did, but she'd never sat next to someone who'd had direct contact with them—who could save her if only she could persuade him to help her. "You must have their phone number then if they said for you to message them."

"Yeah, I've got a special phone I use just for them. George sent someone round to give it to me. He sent another man round, too, but I didn't like him. His name's John, and he was supposed to read to me or do puzzles and stuff, but he asked too many questions and I didn't want him here anymore. But that's okay because Miss Daulton has sorted out the classes at the community centre, so I won't be lonely. I'll be going to those. There was this girl called Sarah there last night, and she's got this thing where she swears when she first meets you, but she's ever so nice and she gave me her phone number, so I think that means we're friends."

"I can be your friend. You don't have to tie me up, I'm not going to run anywhere." That was a massive lie, she would if she got the chance, but she hoped she'd sounded sincere.

"As long as you promise to get in the cupboard when I say so and not hurt me…"

"I wouldn't want to hurt you." *But I'd do it if I had to.* She had to be careful now because he'd mentioned John asking too many questions, and she didn't want to alienate him, but she had to know: "Who's Miss Daulton?"

"She's the lady from the social who looks after me."

"Does anyone else look after you?"

"Mrs Kapor, she's the medicine lady, but she only comes round to make sure I've got my prescriptions and tablets."

"I could look after you if you want."

His phone bleeped, and she leaned across to read the message when he lifted the screen closer to his face.

They've gone but will be back later at two in the morning to collect the cargo. We'll also be there, so don't worry.

Freya's stomach rolled over. "Ask them where they're taking me."

He did that, and the response wasn't helpful at all. All it did was raise her anxiety levels.

No clue, and it's none of our business so long as we get paid. Don't answer the door to anyone.

So that was that then. Unless she could get away, she was stuck here until she was collected. She shivered at the memory of Cool Raffia's eyes through the letterbox slot. What the hell was he doing in the UK? What had he done, picked her as a target when he'd given her the tour? Was there a certain type he looked for? The scarred man on the plane—had he been in the blacked-out van? Had the other one been in there, too, the big one, or did the gang contain more people than she could ever imagine?

"Those men that were outside, I've got a story to tell you about them if you want."

"I like stories."

"We should introduce ourselves first. My name's Freya."

"I'm Eamon, but everyone calls me Puggy."

"What do you want me to call you?"

He shrugged. "Puggy's all right."

She wrapped the quilt tighter around her as a comfort while she launched into the day she'd signed the ledger at the guard hut. And to think that from the moment Cool Raffia had spotted her, her fate had probably been changing to accommodate whatever the gang were going to do to her. She'd been uneasy at the resort afterwards, jittery and suspicious on the plane, and even when she'd got home she hadn't felt right. She wished she'd spoken to Mum and Lottie about what had happened, because at least then the police would have something to go on, because there wasn't a doubt in Freya's mind: her mother and her best friend would have contacted the authorities by now.

She was hopefully being looked for, but there was no way any leads could be found to show she'd been dropped off here unless the vehicle she'd been brought in had been caught on CCTV. It had happened in the middle of the night, and she was sure it had happened to someone else before her because of how smoothly it had gone. These people knew what they were doing, and it scared her to think that her existence in this flat was probably only known by a handful of people.

When she left here, would Puggy and Fish and Chips move on as though they'd never met her? Were the last few days of her life mapped out already? She had no control over it at all unless she could convince the lad beside her to do the right thing. She only had until two in the morning, and considering she didn't even know what time it was now, she couldn't even work out how many hours she had left. She'd been so intent on reading the message he'd got that she hadn't looked at the top of the screen to check the time.

She'd have to remember to ask Puggy, but for now she was more interested in telling him her story and making him see how bad everything was, how awful the men were to have snatched her the way they had. How terrible it was that she was kept here and Puggy was expected to look after her.

She'd play on his emotions, something she didn't like to do to anyone, but she had no choice. She was convinced this was a life-or-death situation, and if she wasn't willing to fight for her survival, then she may as well give up right now.

Chapter Twenty-One

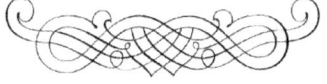

Puggy had made the right decision by not tying Freya to the bed and putting the cloth in her mouth. Like he'd thought, she hadn't hurt him. If he were in her shoes he would have lashed out, but she seemed so calm considering what was going on. It was nice not to think of her as Income, although he still felt guilty because she didn't deserve to have been brought here. He done his best to look after her, to make things a bit better, although he'd never get over having to leave her with a dirty bum. At least he let her use the toilet sometimes.

Her story had hurt his heart, had overwritten his desire to earn pocket money. It had brought his mother to mind. She'd be so ashamed of him for taking this job, and if there was such a thing as Heaven she'd be looking down and shaking her head at him. She'd be shouting and telling him off.

He didn't like the idea of her being disappointed in him, even though she was dead. She'd always taught him to do the right thing, but ever since he'd met Fish and Chips it seemed he was always doing the *wrong* thing. The problem he had was, even though he knew it was naughty, he was doing it anyway. Was that because he didn't have Mum there anymore to show him the right way to go? It was difficult living by himself and having to make decisions. Miss Daulton was great, and she talked things through with him a lot, but it wasn't like he could tell her about selling the drugs and now looking after Freya. Miss Daulton would phone the police on him straight away, and he'd be in all sorts of trouble then.

He might lose the flat and his benefits. They might put him in one of those assisted living places that he'd fought so hard to avoid.

Cool Raffia and Big B. Raffia wasn't very cool if he'd tricked Freya like that in Jamaica, and Big B wasn't very nice if he'd let his other friend punch her when they'd been in her flat. Puggy felt so bad that he was involved in this. He'd known from the beginning that keeping a woman in the cupboard wasn't a good thing and that it could lead to something worse happening to her, but the pound signs had persuaded him to do it, not to mention Fish and Chips being especially forceful.

He hadn't felt like he could say no.

He wished he was a different person, someone who was strong and able to say no. Someone who never had anybody telling him what to do, threatening him. It had happened as far back as he could remember, feeling like people owned him, and he was tired of it.

With no idea in which direction this could go, he couldn't make his mind up on what to do now. He preferred to know what was going to happen, but Miss Daulton had told him that sometimes he could never know what was going to happen because other people's actions affected your life whether you liked it or not. He'd made himself understand what she was saying, and thinking about Fish and Chips and how they'd knocked on his door told him how things were going to be, and that was the end of it. *They* had affected his life whether he liked it or not.

He thought about his options. He could keep Freya until she was collected later, or he could phone for help. It was all going to turn into a mess if he got hold of The Brothers. It would mean telling them Fish and Chips had come back to bother him, and then he'd be in trouble for agreeing to keep Freya here. Especially because they paid him to find things out for them. They'd say he didn't need to earn any more money because he was already earning enough from them—and more if he got his arse into gear and actually told them shit.

They'd call him greedy, and he wasn't sure that would feel very nice.

Should he just ring them and let Freya explain?

And why hadn't Fish and Chips been round yet with his money? Was he going to have to wait until two in the morning?

"I don't want those men to come back for you, but at the same time I don't want to tell on them," he said. "Fish and Chips will be angry, and they'll come here and hurt me."

"Not if the twins get to them first. And isn't it better to tell the twins what you've done than the police? They could charge you with being part of a kidnap plot and you'd go to prison."

His stomach rolled over at the thought of that, all those hideous men in cells, spitting at him and shouting and tripping him over and being mean. He'd watched a telly programme about prisons once, and it looked really scary.

"What if the twins tell the police about me?" He squeezed his bottom lip and twisted it to keep his mind on that rather than the uncomfortable feeling in his chest. Miss Daulton said they were anxiety flutters.

Freya put her hand on his arm. "They wouldn't."

"How come?"

"Because they like to deal with stuff on their own, no police involved."

"What if *they* hurt me?"

"They won't if I talk to them. I can tell them you were forced into it and you told me you didn't want to keep me here and only wanted to help instead."

He *did* want to help, he was just worried how it would work out for him afterwards. Life was uncertain enough as it was without all of this on top. He'd fretted about this job as soon as he'd been asked—or told—to do it, and his doctor had said he wasn't supposed to be getting stressed. He thought about the days before Fish and Chips had knocked on his door, how he thought his life was difficult, but looking back on it now, it had been so easy to only have life in general to deal with, nothing extra.

"If something happens to me after I leave here with those men," Freya said, "you might be classed as having something to do with it. The police will see it as something that's called a joint enterprise, and even though you only let me stay here and weren't horrible to me, you were still involved in the chain of events. Do you understand?"

He nodded, although he'd need a couple of minutes to think through what she'd said properly, because it was a lot to digest. He got up and peeked out of the spare bedroom window, checking the back garden to make sure those men weren't there, or that Fish and Chips weren't spying on him. No one was out there, and it was then he realised he'd forgotten to hang her washing out.

"I won't be a minute."

He left the room and locked her in, taking her clothes and the towel out of the machine then going into the garden to put them on the line. It was a lovely day, and after he'd finished he stared at the blue sky for a while, wishing Fish and Chips had never knocked on his door that first time.

He thought about what Mum would say. *"You should let the twins know what's going on. You've got enough tracksuits and trainers, some of them still brand-new, so it isn't as if you need more, and if the twins believe your story, you could earn hundreds a week by being nosy out the front and finding more information for them."*

Movement in the corner of his eye drew his attention to the spare bedroom window. Freya had pulled the curtain across a little and looked out at him. Her story had been awful, and like she'd said, they could only guess at where she'd be taken next and for what reason. He'd watched a documentary where women were nabbed and sold, and it hadn't been that long ago that a load of refugees had been brought to London by a gang called The Network. It had been in the news and everything. Some of those ladies had died, buried in Daffodil Woods.

He didn't want Freya to die. She was nice, and she said she could be his friend. If he let her go with the men then she wouldn't be able to do that.

He took a deep breath and went inside, locking the back door. He entered the spare room to find her sitting on the bed with the quilt wrapped around her, and it reminded him she needed to get dressed in one of his tracksuits.

"I want you to tell the twins everything," he said. "But I don't want to get in any trouble."

She got dressed beneath the quilt. "It'll be okay. They'll understand you didn't have any choice."

A terrible thought struck him. "But what if Fish and Chips see them come here? They could be watching me. Those other men could be watching, too."

"They can come in round the back."

"We'd better get it sorted soon because I've got to go to the community centre tonight." He didn't want to miss the next class, not when he'd only just been accepted. "Do you think they'll let me?"

"They might want to keep you safe until they find Fish and Chips and those other men."

He nodded. "I'd better go and get their phone, then."

He left the room, once again locking her in, and found the burner in the drawer in the kitchen. While he was in there he pulled the blind down—the thought of anyone looking in twisted his tummy into knots. He joined Freya back in the bedroom and sat by her on the bed.

"I'll put it on speaker so we can both hear what they're saying," he said and opened his contact list, prodding the only number that was in there.

"All right, Eamon?" George asked. "Have you got some info for us?"

"Yes, but you've got to promise you won't hurt me first."

"Why the fuck would we hurt you?"

"Because I think I've done something wrong. There's a lady here, and she's called Freya, and—"

"Hang the fuck on. *What* did you say her name was?"

"Freya, and—"

"Can I talk for a second?" Freya said.

"Are you Freya Duncan, love?" George asked.

"Yes."

"We've been looking for you. We're on our way to the flat now."

"Wait," she said. "It's important that you're not seen coming to the front; Puggy might be being watched."

"Who by?"

"Two men called Fish and Chips, plus another two men. I'm going to briefly tell you what's happened before you get here so you understand Puggy's been forced to keep me in his flat."

"Jesus fucking Christ."

Puggy didn't feel very well. Everything in his head was stacking up and creating confusion, like angry bees buzzing, and he wished his skull had a door so he could open it and let them out.

He smoothed his palms up and down his thighs, over and over, saying, "I only did it for the tracksuits. I didn't mean to do anything bad."

"It's all right," George said. "No need to panic. We'll look after you now. Just sit tight until we get there, okay?"

"Okay."

Chapter Twenty-Two

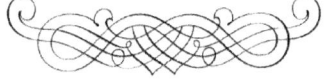

After a quick detour home to put on long wigs tied back into low ponytails, beards and sunglasses, grey tracksuit bottoms, and plain black T-shirts, George and Greg were on the way to Puggy's flat. Although pleased they'd discovered the whereabouts of Freya, George was incensed that Puggy had been coerced into doing something bad yet again. To add to the angst, Greg had a bee in his bonnet in case this was a trick and they'd turn up to find no Freya, just Puggy luring them in for those bastards called Fish and Chips.

A while back, two of their men, Carling and Tez, had received a tip-off regarding Shawnee hiding out at Puggy's flat. She'd been a wrong 'un, disposed of in the Thames, and her nan, Isla, now provided information as a grass and whatever toiletries they needed from the 'supermarket' room in her house. She was a modern-day Robin Hood, providing stuff on the cheap for locals in the know, and by all accounts quite revered. Basically, she'd given her blessing for her granddaughter to be killed in exchange for her own life. Shawnee would have been killed regardless, but it was nice to know Isla knew her place.

George had eventually won over Puggy's trust and persuaded him to explain his part in a bloke called Andre's drug empire. Two men calling themselves Fish and Chips had approached Puggy and asked him if he wouldn't mind storing boxes for a mate of theirs—aka Andre. In the end, Puggy had sold drugs, and he'd maintained that he didn't know who Fish and Chips were, what they were really called, and besides, they always visited him with balaclavas on. Puggy had nothing bad to say about Shawnee; he saw her as an angel who'd helped him manage his life.

"What the fuck do you reckon we're walking into?" George asked Greg who parked their little van in the street behind Puggy's block of flats.

"Like I said, I'm worried this is going to be an ambush."

"So you think word got round that we're looking for Freya, and Fish and Chips are going to use it as an opportunity to what? Kill us? Do us over?"

"I don't know, we just have to make sure we're careful."

They left the van to walk down the alley behind the flats, then turned left to go down another alley. They already knew where this one led because they'd been here before to collect Shawnee. George stared through a knothole in the fence and checked out the back garden. Washing hung on the line, but otherwise there was nothing else going on—that he could see. There was a blind spot to his left. He was reluctant to let Puggy know they'd arrived yet, just in case this *was* a setup, so there was nothing for it but to get in the garden and hope for the best. He turned the handle, but the gate remained locked, so he vaulted over.

When they were both on the other side and George had ensured there was no threat whatsoever in the garden, he nosed through a window. Beyond it, a living room and then the hallway, the front door at the end. The other window had closed curtains, although he swore one of them twitched.

His phone rang, Eamon's name on the screen.

George answered. "I take it you're watching us."

"Why are you answering George's phone, and why do you sound like him?" Puggy asked.

George remembered they didn't look like they usually did and cursed himself for not warning Puggy before they'd arrived. "We've got disguises on so nobody knows it's us."

"We were scared the men had come back, that's why I peeped out of the window when I heard someone at the gate. Then I saw two men with long hair and I thought… I thought…"

"I understand, and I'm really sorry that we frightened you."

Since listening to a brief rundown of Freya's account of things on the journey here, George could understand why they'd be afraid. She'd been followed from Jamaica and then abducted in London, and that was enough to shit the life out of anyone.

"Come and open the back door," George said, "and if you're fucking us about in *any way*, I'll be really angry with you, do you understand?"

"I don't know what you mean."

"Is it just you and Freya in the flat?"

"Yes."

"Right, then come and let us in."

"Fish and Chips told me not to let *anyone* in."

"If you don't let us in, how are we supposed to help you?"

"Me and Freya could come out into the garden."

"But we're going to need to go in anyway to check your flat."

"What for?"

"To make doubly sure no one's in there with you."

"But there isn't."

Despite knowing to go softly with Eamon, George let his temper get the better of him. "Just open the fucking door, will you?"

"Okay."

George stared through the living room window. In the hall, the lad came out of a doorway with Freya in tow. It was such a relief to see her, although she looked drawn compared to the images they had of her. Bruised. Who'd hit her? And that tracksuit looked about four sizes too big. Puggy shuffled over to the back door and unlocked it, putting the keys in his pocket as if it was a deep-rooted habit, then opened up to step outside while his gaze darted around the garden—he was clearly crapping himself, but what did he think was going to happen, the men would materialise out of the fucking fence?

Freya followed him out, and Greg went inside to search the flat.

George raised a finger to his mouth. He didn't want any of what had happened here getting out and into any neighbours' ears—that could fuck things up later on if what he had in mind went to plan. He pulled the bolts across on the gate, poking his head out into the alley to make sure the way was clear. No one was around.

Greg came back out and shook his head—the flat was empty.

"Go and switch on the hallway light so the flat's not dark later, then come back out here and lock the door," George whispered to Puggy.

He did as he was told, unable to make eye contact with George who had so many questions sitting on his tongue it wasn't funny. Greg led the way out of the garden, and George indicated for Puggy and Freya to go next. George left last and followed them down both alleys and into the street where they'd parked the van. Puggy and Freya got in the back—Puggy had brought a bag with his meds and clothes—and with George and Greg up front and their seat belts on, they were on the move.

"Who the fuck hit you?" George asked Freya.

"One of the men who took me."

"Would you recognise him again?"

"Yes."

"So if I ever catch up with them and I send you a picture…"

"I can say yes or no."

"Right."

"Where are we going?" Puggy asked. "I like to know what's happening, I told you that when we talked before."

"To one of our safe houses. There's a man called Will, he'll look after you there." George turned to look at Freya over his shoulder. "We'll contact your mum once we've arrived."

"Thank you."

"Will we be back by this evening?" Puggy asked. "Only, I've got to go to the community centre."

"You'll have to give it a miss. Have you got the phone on you that Fish and Chips use to contact you?"

"Yeah."

"Then you're going to have to give it to me so we can read any messages. If Fish and Chips text you before two in the morning with a change of plan, we need to know. When this is all over, you can have your phone back."

"But what if Miss Daulton messages?"

"I'll answer as if I'm you."

A tut, then, "What are you going to do after you've dropped us off?"

"We're going to make you safe by meeting Fish and Chips and those other men at your flat later.

We'll take them away so they can never upset you again. Then we need a serious chat about the way you earn money. It is *not* okay to sell drugs or to hide kidnapped ladies in your bedroom. We've already had this conversation before when Shawnee stayed there, and you said it wouldn't happen again."

"But Fish and Chips came back even though they said they wouldn't, and they made me keep Freya."

"It really wasn't his fault," Freya said. "He did a lot of things he was told not to, like he took me into the bathroom to use the toilet sometimes, and I was allowed to shower. He fed me properly and made sure I had enough water. He's been cleaning out the bucket he was told I had to use."

"It's okay," George said, "I get that he's an innocent party in all this who's been coerced, and believe me, Fish and Chips will get what's coming to them, as will this Cool Raffia and Big B, but as for the others… Unless the Jamaicans talk to us, then it's probably unlikely we're going to be able to bring the others to justice. I'm thinking we'll have to do an anonymous tip-off to the police with regards to them."

"I don't want anything to do with that," Freya said. "I can't have them thinking I've grassed them up. I'm already worried they'll come after me as it is once they realise I'm not being picked up in the early hours. I mean, what am I supposed to do, just go home tomorrow and live my usual life when there's a risk that other members of the gang are going to abduct me again?"

"We'll know more after the interrogation, but if it's left where the Jamaican gang are still out there, free to do whatever they want to others, then you're going to have to change your name and move away. Is that something you're prepared to do?"

"God, yes."

"Good, because it might well come to that. These bastards sound too dangerous to mess around with."

They drove into the countryside.

"You'll need to put blindfolds on so the safe house remains anonymous," Greg said.

George took some out of the glove box and passed them over. Puggy and Freya complied, and he felt sorry for them. It must be scary to be in their situation, each of them frightened for different reasons.

Puggy hummed some kind of lullaby and rocked for the rest of the journey.

Ten minutes later, after Freya had recalled some more memories that might well help later on when George asked his questions, Greg turned down the track to the safe house that stood surrounded by an orchard in its own grounds, no other homes around. A new acquisition, which George fancied living in himself, but it was too out of the way for them to get to Cardigan quickly if anything kicked off. A shame, because Ralph would go nuts if he saw all this grass.

Will's car was out the front, and Greg parked the van beside it.

"You can take the blindfolds off now," George said.

Everyone got out, and Will came to the front door. George made the introductions, and they gathered in the living room where Will had put some Tesco carrier bags on the sofa containing clothes and toiletries. George took Puggy's phone off him, plus the PIN code, and once he'd checked it worked, he messaged Maria on his own work burner.

GG: Freya found. There will be a phone call from her in a couple of minutes. She'll explain everything. We have yet to round up the people involved and would prefer the police weren't contacted. You'll understand once she's said what went on.

With Freya off in a bedroom speaking to her mother, George ensured Puggy felt comfortable with Will. It seemed they'd hit it off as Puggy was going into quite some depth about how to body pop.

George shook his head and left the house, Greg following. Will would explain anything Puggy or Freya had a problem with, and for now George had to put them out of his mind. They had plans to make. With four men due at the flat, two of them to collect Freya, he felt it best that they took extra hands along. Moody and Jimmy would do, plus Carling and Tez.

He got in the van, clipped on his seat belt, and waited for Greg to do the same.

"I took Puggy's keys off him," Greg said. "We'll need them later."

"Right. We'll go home so I can take Ralph for a walk, then go over a plan. We'll round those bastards up as quickly as possible once we open the front door when they arrive, no fucking about. I want them hanging up in the warehouse cellar by three."

Greg drove away. "I'll nip to the chippy on the way home to get some grub. I've got sausage and chips on the brain."

George nodded absently, his mind a million miles away, on four men who were soon going to regret the day they were born.

Chapter Twenty-Three

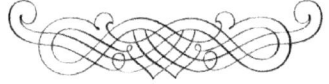

Freya left the pizza shop, the warmth of the food coming through the bottom of the box onto her palms, burning her skin, so she switched to gripping it at the sides. That was better anyway, as she could hold the handles of the carrier bag now instead of having them digging into the crook of her elbow. The wine bottle was heavy, and she also had a large bag of Haribo

in there, never so glad in her life to be paying two-fifty for a packet instead of the extortionate prices abroad. She planned to watch a couple of films, or if she couldn't find any that took her fancy then she'd binge one of the series she'd missed while on holiday.

She crossed the car park, jolting a little at the sight of two black men standing by an old-fashioned car. The men didn't take any notice of her, too busy talking amongst themselves, their backs to her and their heads close together, so she told herself off for worrying that they were here for her.

They could be... The man on the plane, the one at the airport...

Her stupid mind had gone into overdrive ever since she'd been scammed, but she had to remember that not every black person was out to do her harm, of course they bloody weren't. Those men over there were just having a chat, that was all.

She took the road that led home, rushing not only because she was hungry but she didn't like being by herself at night—James had drummed into her head that it was dangerous for women to be on their own, and the fear he'd created had stuck with her. She'd always come here with him before, their weekend ritual to visit the newsagent's for snacks and booze, the pizza place for dinner. She was surprised she hadn't had a pang of longing at the shops for the loss of times gone by, so maybe she really was over him, just bitter still. But that would change the more time that passed, and one day she'd realise she hadn't thought of him that day, hadn't thought of him for weeks, months, and then she'd know she'd reached a good place.

She arrived home and put the pizza and bottle of booze on the side in the kitchen. She emptied the machine and took the washing into the spare room, hanging it over the two empty airers. She had a quick bath, collected her food, drink, and a glass, and took it all into the living room, popping it on the coffee table. The air was a bit stale from the flat being locked up, so she opened the window, a cool breeze billowing the voile curtain inwards.

She switched the telly on, poured a glass of wine, and browsed the selection while eating a slice of pizza. Her phone buzzed, Mum's name on the screen, part of her message visible: ARE YOU OKAY? DO YOU WA

Unable to lie to her, because she wasn't okay, not really, she chose to ignore the text. Mum would reread the last one Freya had sent and eventually get it into her head that she didn't want to be disturbed. She said she wanted a quiet evening alone, and while she loved her mother to death, sometimes she wished she would give her some space.

She found a series and pressed PLAY *on the first episode, settling back to enjoy her evening, thinking only about herself for a change and how good those sweets were going to taste after she'd finished her dinner.*

She woke to darkness and the television off, something it did by itself if she didn't respond to the on-screen prompts by pressing the remote control to continue watching. It was chilly, the breeze coming through the window harsher now, so she got up, intending to shut it. With her hand out ready to do that, she paused at a light tapping sound coming from her front door. She frowned and went to the sofa to find her phone so she could check the time. It was after midnight, so surely Mum hadn't come round, worried because Freya hadn't responded.

She went to the front door, asking, "Who is it?"

"It's the police."

Frantic that something had happened to Mum, Freya snatched the chain across then the bolt, and flung the door inwards. Too late, she saw the police weren't at her door but the two men from the plane and the airport.

The shorter one with the eyebrow scar pushed her in the chest, and she staggered backwards, the inane thought that she hadn't even screamed yet entering her head. She opened her mouth ready to let one loose, then Scar was on her, a gloved hand clamped over her mouth. With the other he gripped her hair and dragged her into the living room by her head, her heels ineffectual in her attempt to dig them into the floor to stop whatever was going to happen next. In the living room, she caught a glimpse of their car parked outside. Had they been sitting out there all night while she'd been oblivious? He threw her onto the sofa and punched her face, the pain of it shooting from her cheekbone to the top of her head.

"Hey, she's not supposed to be hurt," the big one said in a Jamaican accent. He tried to get between his buddy and her.

Scar shoved him away. "Fuck off."

Mr Big stumbled in reverse, his elbow knocking a vase off the windowsill and onto the floor. She prayed the people in the flat below had heard the noise, or maybe someone outside walking past after a night out, or the couple next door, but for an agonising moment or so with Scar's hand over her mouth again, ramming the back of her head into the sofa cushion, there was no sound but their breathing. The air seemed to prickle with menace, the men so still, so clearly adept at this.

Like they'd done it before.

No sounds came from the other flats or from outside.

No one was coming to help her.

"Get this shit off the coffee table into a bag. We'll take it with us," Scar said. "We don't want to leave behind any clues that she's been to the shops."

"But if she used her bank or credit card, then someone will know."

"It doesn't matter, we faced away from the cameras." Scar turned to her and smiled, raising his fist.

The next thing she knew, she was in a moving vehicle after receiving another punch, this one to her temple that had knocked her out. Was she in the boot of their car or on the back seat? She couldn't see where they were going, her eyes were covered, and something filled her mouth, shoved so far back it touched her tonsils. It tasted of oil. She gagged, the pizza, wine, and sweets threatening to come up. Her eyes watered, and

she couldn't lift her hands to wipe them away as they were tied behind her back.

The vehicle stopped, and she held her breath to listen to the sounds around her. Footsteps. Murmured voices. The sharp clunk of a door being opened. She was hauled out then slung over a shoulder. Whoever carried her walked quickly, her upper body bumping against his back. She felt so vulnerable and unsteady, not trusting that he wouldn't drop her. Who were they? What did they want? Mr Big kept repeating that he was sorry and he'd try and make it right, that she didn't deserve to be hurt like this, or treated like this, and if he could find a way to set her free then he'd do it.

She didn't believe him.

The air changed, going from outside to inside, she guessed, and it smelled of pizza, confusing her into thinking they'd taken her back home. But she couldn't detect the scent of drying washing like she had in her flat, and there was another smell here, one she didn't recognise, perhaps the unique odour of someone else's home. It wasn't bad or horrible, just alien. Where had they brought her?

"Where will she be staying?" Mr Big asked.

"In the spare room." London accent. Male.

Oh my fucking God, what the hell is happening?

She remained limp, wanting them to think she was still out for the count. She might find out more this way.

"Are you sure she'll be looked after properly here?" Mr Big again.

"We wouldn't have suggested it otherwise, dickhead."

"Less of the name-calling," Scar snapped. "Let's just get her in there out of the way, then we'll discuss the requirements in the kitchen. She's got a few messages on her phone from her mother. I'll reply to her and then switch the phone off."

"You should have done that before you brought her here," the Londoner said. "That phone could be traced to this location now. Like I said, dickhead."

"If you don't watch your mouth…"

"Stop it," someone else said, another male who sounded young and afraid.

Mr Big carried her, presumably into the spare room, sitting her on what she thought was the floor. She sensed being closed in somewhere, so maybe she'd been placed near the door, but it felt different to that; she had the suffocating sense that the air was about to get stuffy and close in around her. Was the spare room really small, was that it? Or was she in some kind of box? A wardrobe?

A door closed, it must be the one to the room, then came the audible turning of a key. Her stomach sank, and tears came, her nose quickly getting clogged up with snot, so much so that she thought she was going to run out of air as she struggled to draw it through the cloth in her mouth.

Then a calm overcame her, and she took a moment to centre herself. Yes, she'd been taken from her own home and brought God knew where, to stay with God knew who, but if she did whatever they said and bided her time, then maybe Mr Big's promise would come true and she'd be saved.

It was the only hope she had left, so she clung to it with all her might.

Chapter Twenty-Four

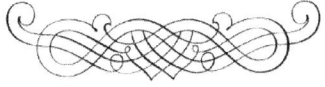

Cool Raffia was *not* happy. Big B had been watching him since they'd got back to the yard behind the supermarket where he'd parked a van similar to the one they used at home when scamming tourists. Raffia drummed his fingertips on the steering wheel, creating a monotonous, irritating sound that burrowed straight into Big B's head, but it wasn't like he was going to say anything, was it. He'd probably get a backhander around the face if he did. Even though Big B's name said it all, that he was bigger than Raffia and most other people, it didn't mean he had the bravado of a bull heading for a rag. He still got scared inside, maybe partly because of his age, but mostly because he was human and Raffia had something about him that was terrifying.

Raffia's phone was lying on the dash, connected via a Bluetooth speaker to Chubby Chandler in Jamaica who was standing in for Digby Dog who had to go to the dentist. Chubby had just asked a question, one which Raffia had yet to answer. He'd told Big B to keep his mouth shut during the call, so he had, but he was dying to clarify what was going on.

"No, I don't think it's going well this time. I'm telling you, whoever our contact is over here, they picked the wrong place to put the cargo and the wrong man to keep an eye on it," Raffia said.

He'd given away the fact that he didn't know everything like he made out. Big B had always been under the impression that Raffia was one of those higher up, despite being used to lure the tourists in. It seemed he wasn't completely in the know after all. "Whoever our contact is" meant he didn't know—or maybe that was his way of letting Chubby know that he wasn't prepared to discuss names in front of Big B.

"So you're dissing our contact," Chubby said. "Disrespecting him for his choice. Accusing him of being crap at his job."

"It's a shitshow here," Raffia blasted out, clearly not picking up on the menace in Chubby's tone.

"What's your specific problem?"

"One, the two men we have to deal with wear balaclavas. I don't like not being able to see who I'm speaking to. They're rude and seem to think they're in charge when it comes to the flat."

"They are. They're paid to make sure the cargo remains looked after there. We don't want her harmed, so our contact will have picked a host who's not so happy with their fists."

Big B nearly blurted that she'd already been hurt by Rudy Dude, her face bruised from punches, but Raffia had told him to keep out of it, so…

But was that the right thing to do, despite being worried about getting a slap? If Big B opened his mouth now and said about the bruises, Chubby would want to know why he hadn't reported it at the time. He'd probably get beaten up when he went back home, but the beating would be worse if he remained silent until someone else down the line saw her bruises and called it in. Then again, he'd possibly get beaten twice, once on his return and once after this phone call, Raffia laying into him because he hadn't stayed silent. But Big B had learned that sometimes you had to take the punishment now rather than later, and anyway, things were going to change. His plan to hide out in Kingston had been growing in his mind until that was all he could think of. He'd get his mother and Sharina out, too. Or maybe it was best they came over here, regardless of whether they wanted to or not.

"She's been harmed," he blurted.

"When?" Chubby barked.

Raffia stared across at him, shaking his head. "I was just about to say that."

"Who the fuck hurt her, Big B, and what have they done?"

"Rudy Dude did it during the abduction. I tried to get in the way to stop it, but he shoved me."

"What the fuck? Don't you worry about him. He's back here now, and I'll pay him a visit after this. He won't be hurting anyone again. How bad is it?"

"Her face is bruised, and the second punch was enough to knock her out cold."

"Shit, and the photos were supposed to be taken tomorrow for the buyer. And what is that *fucking noise* in the background?"

Raffia stop tapping the steering wheel. "It was me. So do we still go and pick her up at two?"

"Yes, the next person who's going to look after is waiting. We don't want to fuck him around, he doesn't like it, if you catch my drift."

"Yeah, man," Raffia said. "I've got a bad feeling about the men in balaclavas, and the boy who's babysitting hasn't got all of his ravens in the treetop. What if he's the type to tell someone what he's been doing?"

"*Tsk*. Our contact trusts the balaclava men, otherwise he wouldn't have chosen them, and in turn, those men trust the boy. Why are you so bothered? Are you offering your services to dispose of them before you come home?"

"It could be easily done."

"*Tsk*." The line cut off.

Raffia stared at Big B. "What were you doing, opening your mouth?"

"Why are you upset about me saying she's bruised? Is it because you wanted to try and get *me* in trouble for hitting her by saying it first? Are you in tight with Rudy Dude and he asked you to blame it on me? Fuck that shit."

By the look on Raffia's face, Big B had guessed correctly. Disgusted, and before Raffia's hand could flash at him, he got out and headed towards the flat, checking behind him every so often to see whether Raffia followed in the van. Five minutes later, with no sign of him, Big B allowed himself to relax, although what he had on his mind meant he couldn't do so fully. He'd likely never relax for the rest of his life, not now he'd made his mind up. And the rest of his life might not be very long.

He reached the flats and strode along the walkway, stopping at Floppy Tits's door, his fist up to knock, but he lowered it when movement flickered behind the patterned glass panel. Maybe she'd seen him walk past her kitchen window and wanted to talk to him about something, because the door opened, and there she stood, beckoning him inside using a crooked finger. He glanced left and right at the other front doors, then turned to stare down into the street. The van wasn't there, so he stepped inside and followed her into the kitchen.

"I was just about to knock," he said.

"Ah, and there's me wanting to talk to you, too. Need a drink?"

"Something cold if you have it." His mouth had gone dry from the decision he'd made, and now he was standing here with this woman, one step closer to actually doing it, his legs went wobbly, so he lowered to a chair at the table.

She took a big bottle of cola from the fridge and poured him a glass, handing it over and then pouring herself one. She left the bottle on the worktop beside a packet of cigarettes and a lighter.

She noticed him looking at them. "Do you want one of those an' all?"

He nodded. It wasn't the good stuff, but it was better than nothing, and he'd left his stash in the flat next door. He lit up, and she opened the window so he could blow the smoke out. That worried him, someone overhearing them—or rather, Raffia creeping along to listen outside. She must be one of those people who were bloody good at picking up on what someone wasn't saying, because she shut the window and pulled a cord in the ceiling for an extractor fan to whir to life.

"What did you want to speak to me about?" he asked.

She joined him at the table. "There's something really bothering you, and I mean more than the average thing that would bother someone. I recognise the body language of someone who's absolutely shitting bricks. You're all tense, like you're *scared*."

"I am, but I'm going to do the right thing."

"Do you want to talk about it?"

"Maybe I should, then I'll know by your reaction what response to expect from the leaders."

"So you're going down that route, are you?"

"Is there any chance I have of staying alive? If they can see why I did what I did, if they're ever lenient…"

"You won't know unless you tell them, but run it by me first."

"It isn't pretty."

"I didn't think it would be. Like I said, I recognise the body language."

He told her about his time in the gang right from the beginning, and going by her expression, she felt sorry for him, thought he was just a dumb kid getting caught up in something he had no control over, but when he'd told her the bit about following some tourists back to the UK and what happened to them here, any sympathy she had dried up. Her face clouded over, and she got up to pour herself another drink, adding vodka to it from a little bottle in the cupboard, then lighting a cigarette and inhaling deeply.

"Shit, I really don't know how they're going to take this," she said, sitting back down again. "There's doing something wrong and then there's doing something wrong, know what I mean? It's way more than I thought you'd tell me."

He nodded. "Will they go easy on me once they find out I did this because of my mum and my sister getting hurt if I didn't?"

She offered him another cigarette. Maybe he looked like he needed it. He took it off her and waited for her to hand the lighter over, but she seemed miles away.

"They might do," she said, then came out of her moment of zoning out. "I heard they were devoted to their mother, and I imagine if anyone had threatened her then they'd have killed them. They might put themselves in your shoes, and all the bad shit you've done aside, and because you're going to them willingly to tell them what's happening, they might not do anything to you. They might be like me and see a kid who's in desperate need of a second chance."

He took the lighter she held out and lit the cigarette. "The problem I've got is them getting rid of me and then the gang doing something to my family anyway."

"Nah. If you ask them nicely, they'd probably make it look like you'd been killed by some random kid in London—then the gang would have no reason to think you'd gone against them, so therefore, there'd be no reason to pay your mum and sister a visit. That's how these sorts of things are done here. George and Greg punish those who deserve it and put things in place for those who don't. If I were you, I'd put it to the twins as soon as you can that you fear for your family's safety."

"So how do I find out where to go to get in touch with them?"

"That's easy, you go to The Angel pub. Speak to a woman called Lisa. She'll get hold of them for you. I'll walk there with you if you like, and I can even stay while you talk to George and Greg. The kids are going to their dad's after school and staying the night. They won't be back till tomorrow afternoon once school's finished. I was only going to do the cleaning then catch up on my telly, but I can do it later."

"Thanks. You didn't tell me before. What's your name?"

"Sharon. And you are?"

"Big B."

"I'm not calling you that. Tell me who you really are."

"Maven."

"Right then, we'll finish these fags and go, shall we?"

His stomach muscles clenched. This was his chance to back out of a confession, to do his bit here then fuck off back to Jamaica, spending the next few weeks robbing tourists until another one was found for them to follow to the UK, then this would happen all over again.

No, he couldn't do it anymore. Better that he confessed than continued to be a part of this.

RAFFIA

Everyone had a limit, and he'd reached his. And anyway, he'd promised the cargo he'd set her free if he could, and he didn't want to fail her.

The Angel reminded him of another pub he'd been in on his last visit to the UK where he'd drank some beer and asked himself what the fuck he was doing. Music played quietly, and people talked loudly. A huge clock on the wall to the right drew his attention. An hour from now it could all be over. He could be dead. How weird to willingly walk towards death rather than run away from it.

Sharon approached the bar and ordered two Cokes from a woman with a name badge on her shirt. Lisa. "Plus we need some help, if you see what I'm saying."

"I'm not asking to be nosy, but what kind of help do you want me to tell them you need, because as you can imagine they're really busy, and they're not just going to drop everything unless it's super important. An emergency on your part doesn't constitute one on theirs, that kind of thing."

Sharon leaned forward and whispered, "People being abducted by a gang from Jamaica. This bloke here, he's got all the information they need to bring the lot of them down. One of the women is currently being held in a flat and needs rescuing. Is that super important enough for you?"

Lisa's eyes widened. "Hang on, I'll ring them to see if they're available."

She put the Cokes on the bar and went through a doorway.

"Are you okay, Maven?" Sharon asked.

"Yeah."

"Even if you were thinking of backing out now, there'd be no point. With the twins knowing there's a gang abducting women on their patch, they're not going to let it go. They'll look into it now regardless of whether you tell them the ins and outs."

Lisa came back. "They're on their way here for chat. You ought to come out the back with me."

Sharon picked up their drinks. Lisa walked to the end of the bar and lifted a hatch, waiting for them by some double doors with a plaque above that said TOILETS. It led to a corridor. She opened a door marked PRIVATE and led them down a narrow hallway that had a camera over the lintel. She knocked on the door and then waved at the CCTV. The door clunked, and she pushed it open, holding it for them to go into what looked like a reception with a tall, curved desk, sofas, potted plants, and some doors that were all closed. The sound of a whip then a screech came from behind one of them.

A young woman sat behind the desk. She glanced up, nodded at Lisa, and then got on with whatever she'd been doing on a laptop. Lisa walked past the desk to a door on the right, ushering them inside. Two sofas faced one another, small tables at the ends farthest away. Maybe this was a little meeting place the twins used for their chats.

Maybe those rooms are where they whip people to death.

Big B shuddered.

"Take a seat," Lisa said, "they won't be long. Oh, and they already knew about this, so you'll likely just be filling in some of the blanks they're not aware of."

She left, closing the door.

"They already know?" he whispered.

Sharon handed him his Coke, and he drank half of it down, then sat on the sofa opposite the door so he could see the twins as soon as they came in. Sharon sat beside him and slapped a hand on his knee.

She squeezed it. "I don't know why I'm surprised that they know. I heard they've got ears to the ground everywhere. I've got a good feeling about this. It'll be okay."

He hoped so, but if it wasn't and he ended up dead, at least this way his mother and sister would be safe—and hopefully, so would any other woman, because he was going to give all the names of all the gang members.

They deserved to go down for what they'd done, so shouldn't he be punished as well? Why should he expect leniency just because he felt bad about what he was doing? He'd done it, plain and simple, and maybe it was best if he was erased. At least then he couldn't be lured into doing something else in the future.

Chapter Twenty-Five

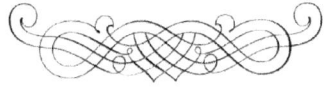

The phone call from Lisa had been a shock and a half, but a welcome one just the same. George and Greg were on the way to The Angel to meet a man and a woman who'd walked in off the street, the woman asking for help, the man standing back and looking a bit cagey, apparently.

He couldn't decide whether he was in the mood to go in all guns blazing with an attitude, so he got the chance for a good old punch-up, or if he should act like an adult and chat calmly. Let's face it, it didn't take much to rile him up anyway, so he might get to lash out regardless.

As Greg navigated the streets, George contemplated the couple's reasoning for coming forward. Had they had an attack of conscience? Were they paranoid someone had seen them doing something they shouldn't have been? Although a woman didn't feature in Freya's story, was the geezer something to do with her abduction? If so, who was the bird, his girlfriend and she'd found out what he was up to and had marched him down to the pub to confess his sins? It wouldn't be the first time a woman had forced a bloke to do as he was told by presenting him to a leader. Then his mind wandered to the utter piss-take of this whole episode, how it had even happened in the first place.

"How come shit like this keeps going on right under our noses and we don't find out about it until ages down the line?" George griped. "I've said it before and I'll say it again, it's like no one gives a shit who we are or what we can do to them when they're caught in the act. These entitled people are going to do whatever they want regardless of knowing they'll be punished for it. Threats don't seem to make a difference these days. It's almost like they'll only believe the promised outcome if it actually happens to them."

"Hmm."

"If you remember, when we were kids, we did as we were told because we were scared of Richard, just like other kids were scared of *their* dads. We knew if we put a foot wrong and he found out about it, we'd get a good old clout. That's what should be happening here, people scared that *we'll* clout them, but nooooo, they're a different fucking breed. Most of them have never been smacked by their parents, and they're all too clued up on their rights, spouting nonsense. It does make me worry that we'll come a cropper one day, meet the person who'd grass us up to the police rather than follow our rules. No one's scared of us anymore."

"Not true, there are loads of people who are scared of us and toe the line. This bollocks happens because there are far too many people living on Cardigan for us to keep a track of, even though we have men and women out there as our eyes and ears. And Lisa said this was a Jamaican gang, so it stands to reason we'd likely not know anything about it. They've probably got family over here who help them get in contact with the likes of Fish and Chips and Puggy. Fucking clever when you think about it."

Greg swerved into the driveway beside The Angel. They got out, and George put the code into the keypad beside the back door that led into reception. A newish bird they'd interviewed the other week sat behind the desk. She helped Amaryllis out from time to time. She called herself Flora, which made him think of margarine. She was pleasant enough and never asked questions. That was a general requirement anyway, but she genuinely didn't seem interested in what was going on. Like now, she glanced up from the computer, saw it was George and Greg who'd come in, then continued with her work. While George appreciated her lack of nosiness, he didn't appreciate her lack of oomph. This business belonged to one of their best mates, and he needed her to be as bright as a button whenever any guests came into the parlour.

"Hello to you, too," he said sarcastically.

Greg closed the door.

She smiled and blushed. "Sorry, I'm trying to catch up on my studies."

Ah, that was it, he remembered now. She was at uni. He felt bad. Maybe she was so far behind she literally didn't have time to make small talk, only deal with the customers.

"How are they going?" Greg asked. "The studies."

"Okay, thank you."

"And how are *you*?" George smiled at her.

"I'll cope." She smiled back.

"If at any time you *don't* think you'll cope, and if you don't want to talk to your parents about the heavy load, then we'll listen or send you to someone who will."

"Thank you."

"I assume the people we're here to see are in there." He jabbed a thumb in the direction of the door to the room Debbie used to use when she'd worked here.

"A man and a woman, yes."

"If you hear any shouting or screaming, just ignore it." George flashed his teeth at her again and entered the room, his gaze latching on to their guests immediately.

The black man, about twenty-three or four, seemed to be crapping himself at the minute, fear in his eyes, his hand on top of the woman's who squeezed his knee. She was white, had gone to seed a bit and looked down on her luck, or if that wasn't what was wrong, she was knackered. Was that from sleepless nights regarding Freya?

George sat on the sofa opposite and waited for his brother to plonk himself down beside him. "Come on then, let's have it."

"Can I just say something first?" the woman said. "My name's Sharon Barker, and I live in the flat next door to the one that he's staying in." She squeezed his knee again. "Maven, that's his name. Anyway, he's only been there a few days, so I don't really know him, but from what he's told me, the poor bastard's been caught up in a gang without being able to walk away."

"What are you, the Go Lenient on Him police or what?"

"I'm not going to lie and say that's not what I'm doing because I am. What I'm trying to say is that even though I haven't known him long and we've only had a couple of chats, I believe him. If he didn't do what he did, they were going to go after his mum and sister, so he had no choice.

And what he's done isn't that bad. It's not like he was the one who punched the girl in the face."

"So you know who hit Freya?" George asked him.

"Yeah. A man called Rudy Dude."

"Are you taking the fucking piss?" Then again, Freya had told them how most of the Jamaicans she'd met while on holiday had two names, but Jesus Christ.

"His real name is Kirk Bax. We all have nicknames."

"And what's yours?"

"Big B."

George's hackles went up, and he had to stop himself from leaping off the seat and launching himself at the bloke—he had to remember that Freya had said he hadn't been cruel to her and had kept saying sorry, that he'd help her.

"So you'll be going to the flat with Cool Raffia at two in the morning then?" George said.

"Not now I'm here, no."

"Oh yes you will, sunshine. You're on our side now, and you'll do exactly what we say. We need everything to seem like it's the same, that it's all going smoothly. Are you any good at acting?"

RAFFIA

"I must be, because my mum and sister don't know anything about what I'm doing—not that I know of anyway. I have to lie to them all the time." He winced.

"Why don't we start with you telling us your story, eh?"

Big B took a deep breath and rested an elbow on his free knee. "It's like Sharon said, I had no choice, but I'll be honest and tell you at the beginning I thought it was the best thing ever, belonging to a group of guys, being accepted, but as more and more things began to happen, I knew I didn't want to do it anymore. By then, I was stuck."

George listened patiently as the whole sorry lot spewed out. "Fuck me, what a mess, but you're going to help clean at least a bit of it up. First, I want all the names and addresses of the gang members in Jamaica and over here. Our police will hear about them once we've dealt with this Raffia fella."

"I'll give you all the ones I know."

George nodded. "Now then, once again, you're going to save your mother and sister, and this is what you're going to do…"

Chapter Twenty-Six

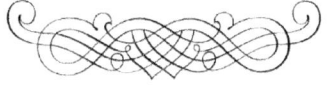

It was a built-in cupboard not a box. She'd managed to push the blindfold off by rubbing her head against the wall behind her. It had taken a while, and she'd been surprised to find daylight seeping in through the crack where the door hadn't quite been closed. Now, she shifted her body around so her toes swept the door fully open. She faced a window with closed curtains.

Daylight seeped around the tops, sides, and bottoms. What time was it? How long had she been asleep before she'd thought of removing the blindfold?

The sound of the key turning in the lock had her gasping, her heart rate going crazy. What if they hurt her because she'd managed to remove the blindfold? If she wanted to keep on their side until she could find a way to get out of here, then she'd have to do something that went against all of her instincts.

A lad came in, snatching in a deep breath at the sight of her in the cupboard with her wrists behind her back. Who was he? What did he have to do with the Jamaicans? Were they good friends? And who was the Londoner? All things she'd hopefully find out if this kid was willing to talk.

He locked them in and put the key in his tracksuit bottoms pocket, then moved closer to her, cuffing dribble from his bottom lip on the sleeve of his light-blue sweatshirt. He cocked his head, studying her, then took a step back as though he needed to distance himself.

"I've got a bucket for you to go to the toilet. I'll bring it in a minute when I go and get your breakfast. I've been told to tell you that if you try to hurt me, then they'll come and hurt you. I'm just looking after you for them so I can get some pocket money. I don't want

to clean your poo and wee from a bucket and I don't want you staying here, but those two are nasty, and I have to do what they say."

Did he mean Scar and Mr Big? What about the Londoner? And now she'd heard this kid's voice, she recognised it as the one who told them to 'stop it' when she'd been brought here.

"You've got to stay quiet, but if you're good, then sometimes I'll take the cloth out of your mouth in case you want to talk. That doesn't look very nice so I think I'll get some socks to put in there instead. If you want me to come in here you have to tap on the wall quietly."

He tugged the corner of the cloth, pulling it out of her mouth.

"I won't cause you any trouble, I promise," she said, "but it would be lovely to go to the toilet." She didn't want to go in a bucket, who would, but she'd do it if she had to. But if he took her to the loo, then she could get some idea of where an escape route was. She had no plans to stay here, and whether her wrists were tied up or not, she wouldn't let that stop her from making a run for it.

He took a long cable tie from his pocket and bit his top lip with his bottom teeth. "I'm sorry, but I've got to tie your ankles. I've got a big list of what I have to do."

RAFFIA

She nodded, stretching her legs out so he could do what he had to do. Never in her life would she have imagined being in this position and allowing someone to bind her ankles, but she was going to play the long game, and if she was lucky, she'd win.

Chapter Twenty-Seven

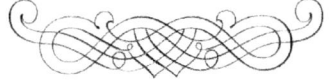

Big B walked back to the flat with Sharon instead of getting a lift from the twins, so if they'd been followed to The Angel by Raffia or one of the others, no one would know they'd spoken to The Brothers.

He let out a long breath. So it was done, he'd broken his promise to the gang and there was no going back. He'd explained to the twins that the police in his town were in with the gang, or at least some of them were, and he wanted to go back to Jamaica as usual before the British police were informed. That way he could move his mum and sister to Kingston and hide them out of the way. Providing the twins allowed him to do that. They hadn't given him any indication of what his fate would be, but they *had* said that no matter what, his mother and Sharina would be kept safe.

It was difficult to have trust in people he'd only just met.

"Was it me," Sharon said, "or did those two smell like vinegar?"

"Yeah."

"It's made me want a chippy tea. I bet that's what they did, had some chips. Shall we stop off at the one round the corner? I've got that envelope George gave me, we can pay for it out of that. That was a fucking turn-up for the books that I got a job off them, eh? I'm glad I went with you now."

Things had worked out well for her; she was now one of their spies. George had seemed genuinely concerned that she looked worn out, and he'd asked about her home life. Her story had spilled out, about an ex who'd got her pregnant twice and then fucked off with another woman, not bothering to pay child support because he had them over at his house for half the week. She struggled on her own as her parents had disowned her for having children without being married, and she'd worked at least two jobs at a time for years.

Big B felt bad for winding her up with the marijuana smoke now. She had enough on her plate, and him adding to it plus dragging her into his mess…but she'd assured him that was okay, *she'd* offered to help, so it was down to her that she was involved, not him.

He'd been told to go round her place for the evening, and that was fine by him. Being alone wasn't a good idea because he'd be stuck with his thoughts.

"If you think about fucking us around once you walk out of this pub," George had said, "like going and telling this Raffia cunt what we've got planned, just remember this: there's always going to be someone half a minute away from you, watching, ready to grip you up and bring you to us."

He glanced over his shoulder to see if they were being tailed. A couple of men were good candidates, although they acted casually, as if they were just walking home from work.

Sharon turned the corner, and Big B jogged to keep up with her. They entered the chippy, the scent of fried fish reminding him of home. Tears pricked his eyes. Jesus Christ, what he'd done in The Angel was so big, something he'd always hoped he would have the courage to do but hadn't believed he could. He'd secured his mother's and sister's freedom, and that would have to be enough. He'd made the right step for them. But whether they would be grieving him in the near future was anyone's guess.

Sharon ordered and paid for the food, cod and chips twice. "We'll get some more Coke while the fish is cooking." She flapped a hand at the woman behind the counter. "Just popping next door, love, won't be a minute."

He followed her into the newsagent's, not wanting to be alone for…reasons. One, if he was never out of her sight then she could vouch for him that he hadn't taken any phone calls or spoken to someone face to face. Two, he didn't want to have to interact with Raffia if he turned up in his van—seeing him later on was going to be difficult enough, and he needed more time to get used to the fact that he was walking the man into a trap. And three, he actually liked Sharon, she was straight to the point and funny, and in another lifetime, she was just what the doctor ordered.

She grabbed two bottles of Coke and took them up to the self-service till, chatting away to the kid putting scratch cards into a plastic case. Then she walked out, Big B going after her. He took the bottles from her, tucking them under one arm, and she gave him a funny look as though he must be from another planet.

"No bloke's ever carried my shit before," she said.

"Then those blokes are bastards."

She shook her head, and he supposed she was thinking he was a contradiction—maybe a gang member with manners wasn't something she'd ever encountered. But you could be good and bad at the same time, because he was, but all the bad he'd done didn't mean he was *actually* bad. Core-deep bad. He'd never wanted to hurt anyone, and maybe now he'd confessed to the twins, all his sins would be absolved.

Back in the chip shop, Sharon was handed a brown bag containing their food parcels, and they walked together towards the flats round the corner.

"Have you got a girlfriend?" she asked.

"No."

"Is that because you've been caught up with the gang?"

"Yeah."

"So maybe now, when you go back home, you could make a go of it with settling down. Find someone nice."

"Maybe. But you have to remember I might not even get to stay alive once I'm back. Who the fuck knows whether the twins have got contacts over there. They could come after me, finish me off because of my part in all this on their patch."

"I didn't get that impression, you know. George wasn't looking at you funny like he wanted to kick your head in, and neither was Greg."

"They might be like Digby Dog and Chubby Chandler, hiding what they're really thinking."

"Chubby Chandler?" A laugh burst out of her. "Bloody Nora." She sobered. "I don't know, I thought they were acting genuine."

They veered round the corner, and he almost stopped short at the sight of Cool Raffia's van parked in front of the block of flats. Instead, he walked faster, ahead of Sharon, saying over his shoulder, "Act like we don't know each other. Raffia's here. If he comes to my door, go into your flat and try to listen to what he's got to say."

With his stomach lurching and his heart beating faster, he moved quickly to the walkway, the bottles of Coke suddenly cumbersome, but at least he had weapons if Raffia angrily approached him before he'd managed to get inside the flat. A whistle sounded, one he recognised as Raffia's, and he stared over the railings at the scary bastard getting out of the van and hop-skipping towards the stairwell.

"Fuck," Big B whispered, conscious of Sharon walking past him with her head down to go into her place. He stood sideways on so he could check whether she kept her front door ajar—he really didn't want to speak to Raffia without her listening. "What's up?" he called out to stop Raffia from coming up the stairs.

Raffia paused and stared upwards. "Thought I could chill with you before we have to go out."

"No, I need to relax and have some sleep."

He noted Sharon's door was open a tiny bit as he strode past and slipped the key into his own front door.

"So I'm not good enough for you now," Cool shouted. "You left the van earlier without a goodbye. That's rude."

More like you wanted to hit me and didn't get the chance.

Big B put the bottles on the floor in the hallway and turned to go back to the railing. "We're not children, we don't have to play these games. I don't want company, I want sleep."

"Where have you been? I've sat in the van for ages waiting for you."

"I went for a walk then picked up some Coke." Big B sucked his teeth and went inside, closing the door.

He stood in the kitchen so he could watch Raffia get back in the van and drive away. Just in case this was some massive trick and he'd been seen going to The Angel with Sharon, and someone else was still out there in a vehicle keeping watch, he took the bottles to the living room and opened the balcony doors, stepping out to lean across and tap on the metal of her railings with one of his keys.

She came out. "Fuck me, I don't like the look of him. He's a sodding rum one, he is."

Big B put the keys in his pocket and passed the bottles over, then gauged the distance, working out if he could jump from one balcony to another.

"My kids can do it," she said, "and they've got shorter legs than you."

He closed the doors that led into the living room and pulled himself up on the railing. Sharon stepped into her flat, then he launched himself across, landing hard, the impact jolting up his leg bones.

They sat in her kitchen at the little table and ate their dinner, both of them getting up every now and again to check whether the van was back. It was going to be a tense evening, but he reckoned she'd keep him calm until he had to go out, as planned with Raffia, at half past one in the morning.

"Would you prefer London over Kingston?" she asked out of the blue.

"I'd prefer anywhere in Jamaica over England. That place is home: the sea, the beaches, seeing the jungle up in the hills. I'd miss the heat. Everywhere here is concrete and grey."

"Not everything, but I get what you're saying. If the twins offered you a job and got your mother and sister over here... What if that was the only way to keep them safe?"

"Then I'd live here. I'd give it all up for them, but I doubt they'd want to leave. Jamaica is everything to them, Ocho Rios especially. It's beautiful. It's going to be difficult to get them to go to Kingston, but at least that's by the sea."

"I bet the colour of the water's lovely."

"Turquoise and blue, and it's *warm*." Talking about it brought a lump to his throat; the memory of walking the private beach by the hotel, going to the end to chat to Cheap Fred, waving to all the locals, the smell of the resort and how the humidity wrapped around him, and the quick downpours that never lasted long in the seasonal months when the tourists converged. The scent of sun cream and mosquito spray and a million different perfumes and colognes. It was so very different to London, so beautiful, lush and vibrant, and such a big part of him, but if it meant he could stay alive, then yes, he'd live in this wet place with its grey and beige landscape and hints of pale green.

And he'd hate it.

"Want to watch a film?" she asked. "It might take your mind off tonight."

He nodded and got up to look out of the kitchen window. "The twins' men are out there, I think."

Sharon went over and stared across the street. As promised, two men sat in an ancient white Transit with an England flag on the aerial.

Big B relaxed.

"It'll be okay," Sharon said. "I've still got a good feeling about this."

They went into the living room, and he deliberately sat next to her on the sofa so that if he got a message, he could lean across and show it to her. Total transparency, which was the complete opposite to how he'd acted before.

And it felt good.

Chapter Twenty-Eight

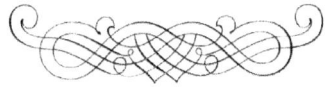

Noel and Joel had spent an uncomfortable evening so far hunched in a smelly stolen Golf with tinted windows parked outside Puggy's flat. Earlier, Noel had the thought that the Jamaicans could turn up there at any minute and snatch Freya away without handing over the second payment. Cue a frantic dash to get a nicked car off a contact, then the drive over there.

He glanced down at the chat group they had with Puggy, needing to remind himself, yet again, that he and Freya hadn't been abducted — and to try and pick up on something that had been bothering him ever since he'd read them earlier. He hated it when there was shit in the back of his mind and he was unable to grab hold of it.

Fish: Are you okay?

Puggy: Yes.

Fish: What are you doing?

Puggy: Sitting with Freya.

Fish: Don't forget to feed her some dinner.

Puggy: I don't need instructions, I've been looking after her fine by myself.

Ah, there it is. Noel had worked it out. Two things. One, Puggy had called her Freya, not Income. Two, he didn't usually give them any lip, so to say he didn't need instructions and whatever, well, it wasn't the norm.

But just because he'd changed his way of texting slightly, didn't mean anything was up. Christ, Noel was getting paranoid. Maybe the stupid thick bastard had let her into his soft-arse heart and that's why he'd allowed himself to use her name.

It was no good, he was going to have to contact him again.

FISH: EVERYTHING STILL OKAY?

PUGGY: YES.

FISH: HAS ANYONE BEEN ROUND? THOSE MEN, I MEAN.

PUGGY: NO.

FISH: ARE YOU STILL IN THAT ROOM?

Noel hadn't caught sight of any shadows breaking up the light seeping through the patterned glass of the front door, but he could have blinked and missed it.

PUGGY: YES.

FISH: WHAT THE FUCK ARE YOU DOING IN THERE?

PUGGY: SHE'S SLEEPING.

FISH: ARE YOU PERVING ON HER?

PUGGY: NO!

Noel laughed and sat up straighter, then felt bad for winding the lad up. Puggy was that dumb he probably didn't even know where to put his dick. Noel sighed. Rubbed his eyes to clear the gritty feeling from them. He'd fall asleep soon if he wasn't careful. They'd had a Chinese takeaway for dinner, and it had made him tired.

Joel had bought the tubs of leftovers with them, saying whenever he had a Chinese he was always hungry later.

He'd better have remembered to bring forks.

While they'd stared mindlessly across the road, it had taken ages for the sky to darken, what with it being June, but even when they'd arrived at eight o'clock, the hall light being on had been obvious to see. The kitchen light was off, though, the blind drawn, and to check whether Puggy was telling the truth about being in that spare room (and not somewhere else, having been kidnapped by the Jamaicans—*stop fucking thinking that!*), Noel had gone down the side of the flats to look through the knothole in the fence. The kitchen light was off but the spare room was on. What had they done in there before she'd fallen asleep, traded life stories?

He chuckled to himself.

"What's so funny?" Joel asked.

"I was just imagining Freya and Puggy having a conversation. I mean, what the chuff would they talk about? It's not like they have anything in common, is it."

"You never know, she might also enjoy doing jigsaw puzzles or whatever the hell he gets up to in there all day on his own."

Noel thought about the stacks of puzzles and board games in the sideboard of the living room. "True."

Joel rubbed both hands down his face. "We don't know her at all. Maybe she's a nerd."

"Not that I even care."

"Me neither."

They resumed staring over the road, Noel a bit peckish. It was after midnight, and there was still two hours to go before Big B and Cool Raffia turned up.

"Did you bring cutlery?" Noel asked.

"Of course I fucking did." Joel reached over to take the carrier bag from the footwell between Noel's feet, passing him an almost full tub of chow mein plus a fork. He opted for the rest of the chicken fried rice, although he'd bought himself a spoon.

They ate in silence, used to this kind of surveillance job, except they weren't getting paid for it, it was their decision to come here to safeguard the forthcoming payment. Once the cartons were empty and stored back in the carrier bag, tossed into the back seat, Noel had another lightbulb moment.

"What if those two wankers turn up without the money?"

"Then we'll have to deal with them—beat the fuck out of them so they're incapacitated. Then we'll take Freya away and keep her stashed somewhere until they pay up—or someone else does."

That wasn't a bad shout, but... "Where would we keep her? We got rid of the lock-up."

"At our place. It's no different to her being in Puggy's spare room. If she's tied up and got her gob full of a rag, and we leave the radio or telly on all day to hide any noise she makes..." Joel shrugged. "Or we could take her to the office flat. Less chance of anyone being nosy there if she manages to make a racket."

Noel was glad their contact had only heard about them via word of mouth and had got hold of them through a friend of a friend of a friend. Only when the authenticity of the Jamaican living in London had been established had Noel handed over their work phone number, which was a pay-as-you-go unregistered effort, the same sort they used with Puggy. Barely anyone knew who they really were. With the careful use of stolen vehicles and the balaclavas, only taking them off when they deemed it safe enough, they'd had the luck of the devil so far—especially when they'd been doing jobs every so often pretending to be The Brothers… Bloody hell, if the Jamaicans probed deep enough, George and Greg might get the blame for helping to hold Freya hostage. But surely that could only mean the promised second payment would be handed over without question. No one would want to fuck with the leaders.

Noel told Joel about his idea.

Joel shook his head, still watching the flat. "If we make out we're those two for this job, we'd definitely get found out by them—and they wouldn't stop looking until they found us, and when they did, we'd be dead. So no."

Noel had expected that answer. He set an alarm on his phone for quarter to two then folded his arms. "That food's made me tired again. Do you mind if I have a kip?"

Joel shrugged. "I'm too wired to sleep. Go for it."

Chapter Twenty-Nine

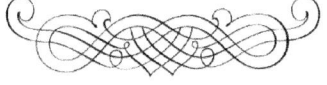

The dark living room in Puggy's flat seemed small with the four of them in it. George, Greg, Moody, and Jimmy waited for the moment either Fish and Chips or the Jamaicans knocked on the front door. If any of them were clever enough, they'd twig the shadow shape coming towards them wasn't the same size as Puggy, but hopefully things would go so quickly that by the time they'd registered that, they'd be on their arse in the hallway, having been dragged inside.

The clock had ticked by so slowly since they'd entered the flat via the back at half past one, but prior to that, there had been the surprising chat with Big B and Sharon, then the plan-making with Moody and Jimmy. Somewhere in there they'd fitted in a snack, and George had taken Ralph out to stretch his furry legs. With ten minutes to go until the rendezvous time, George was getting antsy.

When they'd driven past earlier, they'd seen Fish and Chips—or the shapes of them—inside a battered Golf, watching the flat. It had confirmed what the twins' men, Carling and Tez, had spotted. They currently hid in an electrician's van three vehicle lengths behind the Golf. To anyone watching, the van appeared empty, but they observed the surroundings through a camera set up on the dashboard and another suctioned to one of the rear windows. There had been no sighting of the Jamaicans, but that didn't mean they weren't there. Big B had mentioned Cool Raffia had a van, but the only one out there when they'd driven past was the electrician's.

Big B had messaged earlier to say that on the way back to the flat from the chippy, Raffia had been waiting for him. Raffia said something about spending the evening together, but Big B had refused.

"Remind me to be extra careful when they arrive," George said, "just in case more Jamaicans turn up. I'm almost sure no one would know we've spoken to Big B, but I'd rather not take any chances."

"He could have had his phone tracked since he left for the airport in Montego Bay," Moody suggested.

"But that would only mean they'd know he'd been to the pub," Jimmy said. "Not who he'd spoken to while there." Thankfully, he'd chosen not to wear one of his trademark tartan suits tonight.

"Not if he was followed in there," Greg said. "We spoke to them in a room in the parlour."

"Shit," Jimmy muttered. "And they might not necessarily have heard about the parlour being out the back."

"That was going to be their excuse if they were stopped on the way to Sharon's," George said. "Anyway, Big B and Sharon have been left alone all night, the pair of them have been checking in every hour, as has Will. Puggy got himself upset because of some class at the community centre and he wouldn't shut up about it until Will had phoned up some woman who runs it to tell her he's not very well. Other than that, he and Freya are okay. You never know, this all might go without a hitch. How hard can it be to drag four men into a flat?"

Big B knew he had to pretend he was still on Raffia's side, but George wasn't sure, despite the lad admitting he'd had to learn to lie a lot, whether he had it in him to bullshit for that length of time, all while knowing he'd grassed. He'd fucking better, or George would have something to say about it.

Big B was unaware that George was toying with the idea of letting him go home. That was his hope, which he'd repeated several times, Sharon adding her two pence worth that he could fly back to Jamaica as though he was still part of the gang so he could get his mother and sister to Kingston. It was best to keep the kid wondering what was going to happen; he'd be more inclined to help them then.

George moved to stand to the side of the living room door, poking his head into the hallway. He put his balaclava on, the others following suit. The black tracksuits and trainers rendered them anonymous.

Headlights went past, shortly followed by the work burner vibrating in his pocket.

CARLING: TWO JAMAICANS HAVE GONE BY IN A VAN. THEY TURNED LEFT INTO THE SIDE STREET.

GG: CHEERS.

CARLING: THEY'RE ON THEIR WAY BACK AND PARKING BEHIND THE GOLF.

George passed the phone to Greg so he could read any communications while George was busy at the front door. He itched to move into the kitchen to look out and see what was going on, but the blind had been pulled down, and raising it would be a dickhead move if Fish and Chips or the Jamaicans spotted him. Once they saw he wasn't Puggy, it was game over.

Chapter Thirty

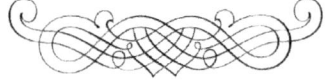

Cool Raffia had harped on at Big B for the whole journey, annoyed the boy—because that's what he was, still a damn boy—hadn't let him into the flat for the evening. Big B had never disobeyed him before, had never disobeyed *any* of the gang members, and it had come as a shock when he had. Raffia expected compliance at all times, and when he'd gone back to the van and driven off, he'd been so angry he'd had to park up around the corner to calm down.

Then he'd messaged Digby Dog, who was still unavailable, so he'd had to make do with Chubby Chandler, who'd said Big B was probably missing home like he always did whenever he went to the UK, hence him being snippy.

CHUBBY: HE DOESN'T SETTLE WELL ANYWHERE ELSE.

CR: SO WHY DOES HE GET TO GO TO THE UK THEN? IT DOESN'T MAKE SENSE TO SEND HIM SOMEWHERE HE DOESN'T WANT TO BE, WHERE HE MIGHT NOT BE CONCENTRATING PROPERLY BECAUSE HE'S MISSING THE FUCKING BEACH. HE WAS WITH A WOMAN, YOU KNOW, SHE LIVES IN THE FLAT NEXT DOOR, OLDER THAN HIM WITH A COUPLE OF KIDS.

CHUBBY: SO? MAYBE HE'S BEEN GETTING SOME LOVING. [LAUGH EMOJI] YOU'RE MAKING A MOUNTAIN OUT OF A MOLEHILL. THE KID WANTS A BIT OF SPACE, HE SAID HE NEEDED SLEEP. SO WHAT IS IT YOU'RE DOING NOW BY TALKING TO ME, TRYING TO GET HIM DEEP IN THE SHIT BECAUSE YOU FAILED TO TELL ME THERE ARE BRUISES ON THE CARGO?

CR: NO!

CHUBBY: THAT'S WHAT IT SOUNDS LIKE TO ME. STAY IN YOUR LANE. I'LL DEAL WITH HIM IF I THINK IT'S NECESSARY. GO AND PICK HIM UP WHEN YOU PLANNED, COLLECT THE CARGO, DROP IT OFF, THEN GO TO BED. YOU'RE BOTH DUE HOME TOMORROW. SOMEONE ELSE WILL BE ARRIVING IN LONDON FIRST THING TO TAKE OVER FROM THERE.

Although Raffia knew full well why the gang operated as they did, using different members for different phases of each abduction, he wished he could see a target through right from when he'd met them outside one of the hotels until they were sold. The way he was only usually used to lure them in had never sat well. But it would never happen. He wasn't that high up, he didn't get to make those decisions, and if he wanted to continue with the status he currently had, then he'd do well to shut his mouth and let his jealousy of Big B fall by the wayside. Why was he jealous? Because the boy was good-looking, could get any girl he wanted without trying, not that he ever did, and he had youth on his side. Raffia had squandered his by smoking too much weed, which had resulted in him walking into traffic and a car driving over his leg, crushing it.

RAFFIA

He stared ahead, shoving those thoughts out of his mind. They sat in the van—they'd done a drive-by to check if anyone was in the cars parked along the road, and he'd spotted the balaclava men behind the tinted windows of a Golf. No other vehicle had anyone in it; he'd imagined them containing either another gang member spying on them to make sure they did their job properly, or someone to do with the masked men.

He got a sense about people, and they were off.

"Check it out," Big B said.

The men in balaclavas got out of the Golf and walked to the rear of the van. There was a knock, then they opened the door and climbed in the back, something that hadn't been agreed on, so of course, it pissed Raffia off.

"I told you to wait for us by the front door," he said. "I sent a message saying it, and I know you saw it because you replied."

"Change of plan," one of them said.

Raffia couldn't tell who was who because of those masks, and the interior was murky as he'd parked between two streetlights. "Eh?"

"We want paying now, *before* we go over."

Raffia laughed. The *gall* of some people. "That's not going to happen."

"Why, because you haven't even bought the money?"

Big B took it upon himself to butt in again, lifting a hand in a signal for them to stop arguing. He leaned forward and took a carrier bag out of the glove box, shoving it between the headrests of the front seats into the man's hands. "Go and put it in your car, then wait for us by the front door."

The men exited, and Raffia stared at Big B, wanting to slap the shit out of him.

"Who the hell gave you permission to overrule me?" Raffia said quietly. "No one, that's who."

"There's no need to play with them. They've done a job, and out of that money they've got to pay that guy who's been looking after the target. Just because you don't like the fact that they wear balaclavas, doesn't mean you can change the rules of what happens in the UK part of the operation. *I've* done this before, *I* know how it works. You haven't, you've always stayed at home, so believe me when I say it's best to hand over what we owe, because we're in a country where we can't pay certain people off if those men went running to them."

Raffia was on the back foot. He hated not knowing what someone meant and he hated feeling as if they had a secret he wasn't supposed to know. "What *certain people*?"

"I've been talking to that woman in the flat next door for a reason, because I heard whispers yesterday when I was in a pub, something about leaders, and when I asked about it, no one would tell me anything. So I asked her, and we went to The Angel for a drink so she could tell me about it. Ask yourself this: when we have Jamaican contacts who live in the UK who'd be in the know, why have we never been told to be careful about the leaders?"

"What the fuck are leaders?"

Big B explained, and Raffia had a horrible sinking feeling that he was seen as being on the same level as Big B, not important enough to know about leaders. It wasn't as if either of them would have refused to come to London had they been told, but it would have been nice to be warned that not only did they have to watch for the police on their backs, but two big men the size of garden sheds. His heartbeat stuttered, and he stared across at the men standing at the front door.

Two big men.

His skin turned cold. "What if this is a setup?" Raffia explained his suspicions. "What if that's why they're wearing balaclavas? As leaders, their faces would be well-known around here, so they'd have to cover them. What if one of our Jamaican contacts is in with them and has told them about us and they've been watching us the whole way regarding this target? Fuck!"

"We have to take the risk and go ahead. We've got orders to collect the target and move it on. If we don't, we're going to be in the shit back home. The next person along the line isn't someone to mess around with, we were told that. If he's expecting us to drop her off in half an hour, then we have to do it, no matter what."

Raffia side-eyed him. "What do you mean, no matter what?"

"If we have to kill the balaclava men, even if they turn out to be leaders, then we do it, take the target to the address, then fly home tomorrow."

If they'd been in Jamaica, Raffia wouldn't be against killing someone. There was the jungle to hide the body, plus the police on their side, but here it was too dangerous, and if the leaders were as fearsome as Big B had said, there would be uproar. People might come to Jamaica to find them for murdering such prominent people.

"No, if it turns out we're being tricked, we don't kill them," Raffia said. "We run. We'll contact home and ask what we're supposed to do next."

"I'll do whatever you say."

"Good. Come on, let's go."

Chapter Thirty-One

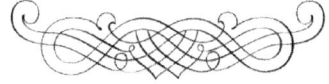

Noel was getting pissed off with that Raffia bloke. A fuck-off big red flag kept waving every time he had to speak to him. Still, they'd been given the money; they'd flashed a special light over it in the boot of the Golf to check for any fakes. It was clear, all of it, and now all they had to do was pass the cargo over, stay with

Puggy for a bit to make sure he was all right—something Joel had suggested they do as a "nice thing"—and then fuck off home.

The Jamaicans were walking over the grass towards them, and Noel braced himself for some argy-bargy. He had a feeling something was going to kick off, and he'd bet his last quid it would be Raffia who started it, the knob.

They'd agreed that Noel would go into the flat first to get the cargo because they didn't want any funny business going on with Puggy. Much as the kid got on his tits, he didn't want to see him hurt in any way, especially because Big B was fucking big. Noel would make sure Puggy was okay and safe in the spare bedroom with the door locked, and then he'd take the woman to the front door.

He couldn't give a shit where she went after that. She was part of a job they'd had to do for a pay packet, nothing more. He suspected she was going to get sold somewhere down the line, and he reckoned she might be pretty underneath the swelling and bruises, so she'd fetch a fair whack.

Whatever, it was none of his business.

"I'm just going to text the lad to make sure he's ready," Noel whispered. "Last we heard she was asleep, so he's going to need to wake her up."

He sent the message, sure he heard Puggy's phone bleeping quite close to the letterbox. Maybe he'd left it on the shoe cupboard by the front door.

He took a deep breath and waited for the response.

PUGGY: COMING TO THE DOOR NOW.

Chapter Thirty-Two

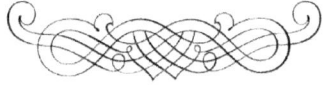

George yanked the door open and gripped the first person he set eyes on—one of the balaclava men. He shoved the bloke behind him for Greg to deal with, then reached out a hand to snatch at the gimpy-legged Jamaican who dithered in place as if his mind hadn't caught up to the commotion, the divvy-arsed twat. Big B and the other balaclava man lunged forward as if to help Raffia, the scuffling of feet on the ground sounding extra loud in the peace of the early hours. Someone grunted, another swore.

George was about to punch the fuck out of someone in order to calm things down, but at last, two dark figures emerged from around the side of the building. Jimmy and Moody. They rushed up behind Big B and Balaclava Two, gripping the backs of their tops and wrenching them away. George all but threw Raffia inside, then Moody and Jimmy marched the other two into the flat. George gave a thumbs-up to the van Carling and Tez were holed up in. They emerged from the back in balaclavas and ran over.

With everyone inside and assembled in the living room, the curtains shut and the light on, George assessed the scene. That fact that all but two people had their faces covered gave him a thrill. Only the Jamaicans had bare faces. Jimmy held a stock-still Big B by the upper arm; Moody gripped a struggling Raffia, Tez on his other side, fingers clamped around his skinny wrist in an attempt to keep him still; Greg had one of the balaclava men in a headlock; and Carling pointed a pistol at the other who didn't appear to want to run or cause any trouble. Maybe he was biding his time before he made a move.

George took a gun out of his waistband and aimed it at Raffia, giving him a lovely wide smile, although he didn't feel in the slightest bit fucking jolly. "Keep still or I *will* shoot you."

"Leave him alone," Big B said, keeping to his role like a good boy.

"Shut the fuck up," George snarled.

Raffia calmed down, his struggles ceasing, although he still looked like he could spit fire. It was all too clear that he liked to be in charge, and now that he wasn't, and it was obvious he wasn't going to be able to escape, his temper crawled out of him to settle on his face in an expression of hatred. "Who are you? All these pussy English people with their masks… Can't even face me like true men. I want to know who you all are."

Who did this little bastard think he was, dishing out orders?

"That's something you don't need to know. What you *do* need to know is that the target, as you refer to her, was removed from this flat earlier today and is now in a safe house. The other thing you might want to know is that you're not going to make it home. We've heard about you and what you did to her in Jamaica, and you're going to have to pay for it by giving up your last breath on British soil."

"Get the knife," Raffia said to Big B.

"I didn't bring it!"

Raffia looked like he wanted to explode, his last chance at salvaging this situation dissipating before his ever-widening eyes. What did he expect Big B to do, stab Jimmy and then turn the knife on everyone apart from Raffia?

Probably.

"Knock him out," George said to Moody on a sigh, bored of the stick-thin twazzock now.

Moody left Raffia in Tez's capable hands and reached into his pocket for one of the four syringes they'd shared out between them—one for Big B just in case he turned rogue on them, but so far it didn't seem like it'd be needed. Moody prepared it ready for plunging, then jabbed the needle into Raffia's shoulder. Raffia shouted out a startled noise of pain, and Tez slapped a hand across the man's mouth. They were all aware of there being a neighbour next door and one above.

The shock on Raffia's face said it all, his mouth open ready to spew God knew what expletives, but the twins' dodgy doctor had assured them that the concoction would work quickly to knock them out but likely only keep them asleep for an hour.

The balaclava men, who'd been quite well behaved, considering, stared at Raffia sinking to his knees, Tez letting him fall to the floor and bang his head.

"That'll leave a bruise," Carling said.

"Are we all on the correct page now?" George asked. "Or does someone else want to naff me off?"

No one said anything.

"Take their balaclavas off," he said to Greg and Carling.

They revealed Fish and Chips. George stared at two men he'd seen knocking around the Cardigan Estate before, ones he'd made it his business to learn the names of because they were young, they had gym bodies, and they might turn out to be trouble. As no word of them creating merry hell had ever reached him or Greg, George had completely forgotten about the pair.

Until now.

Carling cocked his head at them. "I fucking know you."

"They're the two who told us about Shawnee being here," Tez said.

Had they shit themselves in the pub when Carling and Tez had approached them for information? Had they crapped it once they'd realised they worked for The Brothers? Had they given up Shawnee's location to get heat off them? Because as far as George and Greg were aware, and going by what Puggy had told them, Fish and Chips had been up to their neck in the drug business with Andre.

These bastards have been working right under our noses. How come we've never seen them on the Estate in balaclavas? How come no one else has got hold of us to tell us two masked men are prowling around?

Something didn't add up here, but he'd find out what it was at the warehouse.

"We've been looking for you. Fish and Chips, isn't it? Well, that's what you're known as to Puggy. To me you're Noel and Joel, two twunts who drink in the Shag's Nest. I heard you're twins, but you don't look like it to me. Then again, you could be unidentical. But that's not important. What is, is that you'll no longer be able to help people like Shawnee and the Jamaicans shaft Puggy and the likes of him. How many other people do you treat like shit? Don't bother answering, I can imagine—especially if you've been going around with your faces covered. Now then, it's time for you to go to sleep, and when you wake up, we'll have a nice little chat. Night-night."

More syringes came out. Noel and Joel were injected, everyone watching for the stuff to take effect. It took slightly longer than it had for Raffia, likely because they were bigger and taller, but they sank to the floor in the end, one of them asking, just before his eyes closed, why Big B hadn't been injected, too.

No one responded.

George took his phone from Greg and sent a message, asking for as much information that could be gathered on Noel and Joel. As he most definitely didn't want them coming up in any police searches, he didn't bother asking Colin or Anaisha for help, nor did he ask their private detective, Mason. Instead, he chose the newbie on the block. A hacker, Moody's cousin. Bea was twenty-two and had started working for them three days ago.

Fucking good timing.

George looked over at Big B. "We're not going to get any trouble from you, are we?"

The lad shook his head.

"Good, then you can help by carrying this toothless cunt to the van." George pointed at Raffia.

Everyone else got busy. They needed to be at the warehouse within the hour to avoid any groggy wake-ups en route. After tying wrists and ankles, they left via the back way, going as quietly as they could down the alleys, their boots scraping on the ground far too much for George's liking. Once Carling and Tez had loaded Noel and Joel into the back of the stolen Transit parked in the street behind the block of flats, they jogged off to the electrician's van, their part in this over.

Big B dumped Raffia inside.

The drive to the warehouse was made at a sedate pace, everyone keeping on their balaclavas, George and Greg in the front, Moody and the rest in the back.

"You did well," George called over his shoulder to Big B. "Did you get anything out of Raffia that we need to know?"

"No. I know the PIN for his phone if you want to read any of his messages."

"Right. Have you been contacted by anyone *at all*?"

"No."

"Is that normal at this stage?"

"Yeah. They'll be waiting for us to let them know we've taken the target to the next person."

"Read through Raffia's messages for me."

Big B did that. "He's had a conversation with Chubby."

"What's been said?"

"He's complained about me not wanting to spend the evening with him. He said I was with a woman and that she lives in the flat next door. It's almost like it was said in a conversational tone but to me he's implying Sharon might be a problem. He's said she's got kids. I don't like that they might get hurt."

"I'll message Tez and Carling to go round and pick her up. Shame, they're probably just about to get into bed." George chuckled. "She said earlier her kids are at their dad's, didn't she, so at least they're safe. We'll get her to one of our hideouts and sort something for her after that. What else was said?"

"Chubby asked if Raffia was trying to get me in trouble, like getting me back because he didn't tell Chubby that Freya had bruises, I did. Then he was told to stay in his lane and get on with things until it's time to go home tomorrow."

"Okay, switch his phone off, because now you need to use yours to message whoever and say you've been tricked by the balaclava men. They've killed Raffia and taken his body, Freya, and the rest of the payment with them. You managed to run away and you're driving back to the flat."

Big B's face glowed from the light of his phone as he sent the message. A couple of minutes later, his mobile rang. He must have put it on speaker, because someone shouted:

"What the *fuck* is going *on*?"

Big B had said he'd learned to lie, but fucking hell, he was really going for it now, likely with his mother and sister in mind—he had to give the performance of his life to save them. He spun a beautifully believable story, so much so that if George hadn't been there to see nothing of the sort had happened, he'd think the whole lot was true.

"Shit, I'll get onto our Jamaican contact in the UK to find out who those men are, exactly," the bloke on the other end of the line said. "Raffia did say he didn't trust them. Shit, why didn't I listen?"

"I don't know, Chubby, but they're fucking dangerous, they acted like *maniacs*. They sliced Raffia's *throat* right in front of me. I'm sick to my stomach, man. I need to get home. This is getting too dangerous."

"Calm down. Just board the flight as normal tomorrow. We'll sort everything else out."

"But what about the person we were supposed to take the target to? You said he wasn't nice. Does he know I'm staying in that flat? Would he come after me as if it's all my fault?"

"Like I said, calm down. I'll contact him, say there's been a complication. Ditch the van before you get to the flat. Set it on fire. Then go and get some sleep."

"Okay. Okay. I'll speak to you tomorrow."

The line cut off.

"Fuck me, it's all go," George said. "I'll have to wake Dwayne up and get him to go and nick the van from outside the flat."

"There's that money in the boot of the Golf, too," Big B said.

George nodded and sent a message. "Where does this UK contact live?"

Big B told him the address.

"Cheers, we'll need that later down the line for the police."

The rest of the journey continued in silence.

Chapter Thirty-Three

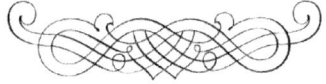

Because Sharon had heard all about the Jamaican gang and the crap going on regarding that poor kidnapped girl, she'd found it difficult to sleep. She'd dozed on and off for hour-long blocks at a time, then stayed awake for about thirty minutes, staring at the gloomy ceiling and listening for any sound that wasn't the norm. She kept imagining someone scaling the balcony and breaking in to murder her for becoming involved.

It was creepy here without the kids, but fucking hell was she glad they weren't at home. Even though their dad was a prick, at least they were safe with him.

She rolled over for the umpteenth time, facing the glowing green numbers on the clock sitting on the set of drawers next to the bed. It was quarter to three. Sodding hell, would this night ever end? To pass the time and hopefully drift off again, she thought about Maven and how he was getting on conscience wise, betraying a gang he'd known for so long. Even though he'd made up his mind to do it, it still must be hard, almost like going against family.

It was no use, she was wide awake. Giving up on sleep, she rolled out of bed and opened the curtains a chink, staring out onto the street behind the block. No one appeared to be loitering around, but there were patches of shadows down there where anyone could be hiding. She shivered, having scared herself, and moved into the kitchen, glad the Venetian blind was closed so no one could go past on the walkway and nose in at her drinking a cuppa at the table. She made some tea, stuck it on a coaster, and parted the blinds to look down at the road.

Someone was getting out of a van. Two someones. One had a flat cap on like in *Peaky Blinders*. At the same time that she jumped from fright, the message tone went off on her phone.

GG: IT'S ME, M, ON G1'S PHONE. HE WAS GOING TO MESSAGE YOU, BUT IT'S BUSY HERE. MEN ARE PICKING YOU UP TO TAKE YOU SOMEWHERE SAFE. JUST A PRECAUTION.

You what?

Her hands shook as she typed a message back.

SHARON: WHAT DO YOU MEAN, JUST A PRECAUTION? WHAT'S HAPPENED?

GG: I LOOKED AT A CERTAIN PERSON'S PHONE ON THE WAY HERE, AND YOU'VE BEEN MENTIONED IN A MESSAGE, SAYING I'D BEEN WITH YOU AND YOU LIVE NEXT DOOR. I'M NOT HAPPY ABOUT IT, AND G1 SAID THERE'S A PLACE YOU CAN GO AND STAY TO BE ON THE SAFE SIDE.

SHARON: WHAT DO THESE MEN LOOK LIKE, BECAUSE TWO BLOKES PULLED UP OUT THE FRONT JUST NOW. CONSIDERING THE TIME OF MORNING, IT'S FUCKING DODGY.

GG: One has a cap on. They're called Carling and Tez.

Sharon: I'll need something more than that, a password. Unless they say it, I won't be letting them in.

A few seconds passed, then Maven sent the word. It was unique, and she idly wondered who the hell had thought of it. She quickly took a swig of tea, lighting a cigarette afterwards to calm her serrated nerves. The steady thud of footsteps on the main stairs gave her stomach a violent lurch, and she inched to the kitchen doorway, puffing away on her fag.

Shapes appeared on the other side of the glass in the front door, one shorter than the other. One of them knocked, and even though she'd been expecting it, she all but crapped her pyjama bottoms. Her heart rate picked up speed, and she laid a hand on her chest, which surprisingly gave her comfort. Her mother used to do that to her when she was a child and had nightmares.

Another knock, then the letterbox flap tapped where it had been lifted. They wouldn't be able to see in because she had one of those draught excluder brush things the postman had to push the letters through.

"There's a password," she said. "What have you got for me?"

"Halitosis."

Never in her life had she thought that someone telling her they had bad breath would make all the stress of this middle-of-the-night adventure go away, but it did, so bloody much. Nevertheless, she needed more.

"What are your names?"

"I'm Carling, and he's Tez."

Satisfied, she nipped back into the kitchen to flick ash into the saucer on her table, took a hefty drag, then stubbed the cigarette out. She undid the bolts and chain and opened the door, giving them the once-over as they walked in. They both had suits on, but the one in the cap had a watch fob and chain attached to his chest pocket, so he looked more dapper. She imagined them walking around the Estate, asking questions and getting answers for The Brothers—and by the look of them, they'd get what they were after, too.

She shut the door and slipped past them where they stood cluttering the hallway. In the kitchen, she picked up her tea. "Do you two want one?"

Cap Man shook his head. "We've been told not to hang around. Go and pack some stuff for a couple of nights."

"A couple? But what about my kids?"

"That will be sorted. When are they due back here?"

"Not until the afternoon, after school."

"Plenty of time then. They can be collected to go and stay where you'll be taken. I don't want to be rude—"

"—which means you will—"

"—but can you bloody hurry up?"

She didn't like the urgency. What did they know that she didn't?

Defiant, fighting against being told what to do, she drank two more sips of tea, staring at them over the rim of the cup. But now wasn't the time to show she could be authoritative, so she went into the bathroom to brush her teeth and collect her toiletries. In the bedroom, she got dressed, packed a bag, collected a few things for the kids, then joined the blokes in the kitchen.

"Once you're in the van, you have to put a blindfold on," Cap Man said.

"A what?" She'd heard him all right, but...

"The place you're being taken to is a hideout, which needs to be kept a secret."

"Fine."

They all left the flat, Sharon clutching her phone. It vibrated in her hand with an incoming call.

"Hello?" she answered.

"It's George. I've only got a quick minute, so listen to me without interrupting. Because we don't know whether the gang think you're a problem, we're moving you to a safe place for two nights and then into one of our flats. It's on the ground floor so it's got a garden, and there are three bedrooms instead of the two you've currently got. Same rent as what you're paying to the council, and we pay the community charge on our properties, so you just have the electric and gas and whatever. I realise you won't want to leave your home but—"

"But I do. I fucking hate that flat. Anything's got to be better than there."

"Then it's sorted, and there might be a new job in the offing an' all, running a café for us—or earwigging while the staff run it. Anyway, we'll chat about that another time. I'll send someone over to your gaff now to empty it and put the furniture into storage. The flat you'll be having isn't quite ready yet because we want to get someone inside to give it a lick of paint throughout. Get some kip in the safe house—either Carling or Tez will stay with you. Got to go. Bye."

She stared at the screen for ages, long enough for it to darken, and thought about having a garden and the extra bedroom so the kids didn't have to share. Newly painted walls that didn't have mould on them. There'd be less fighting between the children, and they'd be happy to be able to go outside and play. Then there was the job, the guarantee of money coming in, enough that she wouldn't have to struggle anymore.

She blessed the day Maven's weed smoke had drifted through those balcony doors. If she hadn't gone round there and had a go at him, her fortunes would never have changed. She smiled that Lady Luck had finally blown a kiss her way, but it was soon doused with worries about Maven and what he'd need to go through once he'd gone home. Explaining to his mum and sister what he'd been doing all these years. Convincing them to move to Kingston. Then holing up there while the gang was arrested after the British police had been in contact with their Jamaican counterparts. Maybe Maven and his family would have to change their names, surely that would be the safest option.

She knew how that went. She hadn't always been Sharon Barker.

Chapter Thirty-Four

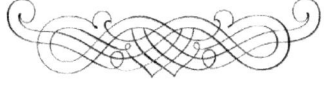

George had been working out in his head what the fuck he could do to help Big B get away from this gang once he was at home in Jamaica. If the kid was staying here and his mum and sister were coming over to live, it would have been a hell of a lot easier. He'd get their names changed, pop them in a flat, give them jobs, sorted. But Big B didn't want to stay in London, so the only alternative was to send him back, which made sense when it came to him maintaining his allegiance to the gang for long enough to get them to believe he'd had nothing to do with Raffia's death and Freya's second supposed abduction via Fish and Chips.

Big B getting on that flight meant the gang could trust him. No one knew his part in grassing them up. To all intents and purposes he'd be safe in Jamaica—except if he told them he wanted to leave the gang. It was better that he just disappeared, so changing their names and living in Kingston... George was prepared to give the lad the money to keep himself and his family safe—he could have the payment given to Noel and Joel. While Big B had done some things he wasn't proud of, things George would normally kill someone for, at least he'd come clean now and a whole lot of wrongs would be righted.

Basically, George believed the lad when he'd said he felt guilty and wanted to get out of gang life. He reckoned Big B deserved a second chance. It couldn't be easy in Jamaica, growing up poor, grabbing whatever chance he could to make a dollar. Christ, there were kids doing it in London, all over England, wanting to belong to a culture, even though they knew it was as rancid as a can full of maggots. What these children didn't know was that you couldn't just dip your toe in, it had to be the whole foot, then the whole body, and if you weren't prepared to give your all, then you soon realised you were dispensable, and being stabbed to get rid of excess baggage had become the norm.

George shivered, aware he and Greg could have gone down that route, but they hadn't, and here they were, in the cellar of their warehouse, Noel and Joel hanging from chains over the trapdoor in the floor. Raffia had been tied up and sat in the left-hand rear corner, Jimmy beside him. Big B, still playing his part for now, sat on a foldout chair near the tool table, bookended between Greg and Moody.

"So, what have you two been up to?" George asked the siblings.

They'd woken around ten minutes ago to find themselves dangling on the chains, confusion and panic the first two emotions, a flash of anger the third, and when they'd realised where they were and who stood in front of them, their minds must have zipped them right back to Puggy's flat and how they'd been captured there. Now, they looked disgruntled but perhaps ready to talk.

"What do you mean?" Noel asked.

"Exactly what I said, what have you been up to, but if you need me to be more specific, what I want to know is what you do for a living and how you've got away with it for so long without us knowing. Puggy has said that you walk around in balaclavas as though it's normal. How come none of our residents have come up to us and told us there are scary fuckers prancing around the Estate? It doesn't make sense to me, and when things don't make sense to me, that means I need answers, and if I don't get answers then that means I'm going to chop your cocks off first, then move to other protruding parts of your body, like your nose and ears and lips and fingers and toes and bollocks, and I'm going to cut them all off one by one until you tell me what I want to know. To save yourself a hell of a lot of pain, just tell me now, because you're going to die this morning, so whether it's in fuck-off pain or not is up to you."

Noel glanced at Joel who nodded.

"We don't want to die," Noel blurted, "so can we make a deal?"

George had no intention of doing so, their lives were ending no matter what, but in order to get what he wanted, he was prepared to lie. "Okay, you tell me what I need to know, grovel with an apology, and then you'll be banished from London. Not ideal for you but better than being eaten by the fishes, wouldn't you say?"

Noel nodded so quickly it was laughable, but George kept a straight face. Christ, this bloke actually thought he was getting away lightly.

"Go on then," George said, "before I change my mind."

Noel looked like he wanted to be sick, or maybe he expected a battering for what he was about to say and needed to gear himself up to receive it. "Um, err, we've…we might have let people think we were you and Greg."

George digested that for a moment, barking out a laugh of…of what? Incredulity? Admiration that they had the balls to even do that? Or was that laugh the precursor to him flipping his fucking bastard lid? Anger surged, so yes, the latter, and he battled to keep it contained. For now.

He cleared his throat. "I see. So you've been going round in your balaclavas, telling our residents that you're us."

"Yes."

"And what have you been doing while you're us?"

Noel peered at his brother again, then stared at the stone floor. "We might have beaten a few people up, threatened them, got them to do what we wanted otherwise they'd get a Cheshire or be kneecapped…"

"So you really went for it, did you?"

"Yes."

"How did it feel to steal our identities? Did it make you feel powerful? Or did it feel like you were complete failures because you had to pretend to be someone else in order to get people to obey you. Doesn't it chap your arse that you weren't good enough to do this in your own names?"

"We didn't pretend to be you *all* the time," Joel said, indignant.

This twin, at least, didn't like the idea of them being seen as less than or incapable.

"So why didn't Puggy think you were us? Why did you call yourselves Fish and Chips for him?"

If Noel could have shrugged he probably would have, but it would be difficult while hanging from chains. "I don't even know why I picked those names."

"So does the Jamaican gang think we've been helping them?"

"No, we didn't dare use your names for this job."

"That's something then, we won't have a load of them knocking on our door, so to speak. Okay, I've heard enough from you two. We'll get you lowered."

Which wouldn't be in the way they thought, but George wasn't about to enlighten them as to their fate, he'd prefer to see the realisation on their faces as it happened. He walked over to Greg and whispered his plan, leaning back to read his brother's expression. It was clear he was surprised that George wouldn't be hacking the shit out of these two, but at the same time he likely wasn't surprised at the method George had chosen to end their lives. Even without blood being spilled, it was a fucking nasty way to go.

Greg opened the trapdoor. George studied Noel's face—a frown, eyes darting left and right, then downwards to the noisy water below. Greg turned the handle to lower the chains, and the unidentical twins dropped, the dopey pair thrashing around as though they could free their wrists from the manacles. George stared down, enjoying the view of their bodies slowly being immersed in the cold water. The chains jangled and clanked, and just as Joel let out a scream for help, their contorted faces disappeared beneath the surface. Two more turns of the handle later, the men covered right up to their elbows, and Greg stopped, coming over to stand beside George while they watched.

Noel and Joel didn't thrash around now. Their forearms remained completely still, as did their fingers. George imagined they were conserving energy. Perhaps at the moment they held their breath, thinking that at any second they'd be hauled back up to beautiful oxygen, but they were going to twig that if they weren't pulled up soon, then George had gone against his word and they were going to die.

It didn't take long, maybe a minute, maybe a bit more, and then the jerking of the arms and the flickering of fingers began. The panic had now set in. One of the faces popped up, Joel's, where he'd used his wrists to push against the manacles, enabling his head to breach the surface, and George had to give it to him, he was a resourceful little bastard.

George glanced at Greg who understood the silent request and went over to the handle on the wall to give it a couple more turns, enough that no amount of pushing on those manacles would raise their faces so they could breathe in life-affirming air. The chains, all four of them shaking violently, filled the cellar with a tinkling melody to accompany their deaths. It echoed off the walls, creating even more noise, and then suddenly, Noel's chains ceased moving. Joel had had the luxury of taking a deep breath when his head had popped up, so he may have another thirty seconds or so left before more water entered his lungs.

George stared over at Raffia who appeared shaken and afraid, and so he should be.

Joel's chains stopped making a racket. The silence apart from the churning water seemed to throb, encompassing them all in a strange, cocoon-like embrace. George didn't like it, it was unsettling, so he clapped loudly.

"We'll have a coffee break, shall we?" he said.

Jimmy gripped a wide-eyed Raffia and marched him up the stairs. Moody held the top of Big B's arm for show, gesturing for him to follow the other two. George remained behind with Greg so he could tell him his plan for Big B.

Greg nodded. "I'm glad we're letting him go. He deserves a second chance."

George patted his twin on the shoulder and mounted the stairs, looking forward to a nice cuppa and a chat around the table.

Chapter Thirty-Five

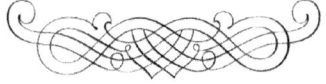

Raffia had witnessed murder, but that episode down there in the cellar… George, a leader, who'd introduced himself and the others when they'd first arrived at the warehouse, had watched those men drowning with such a detached air that it reminded Raffia of himself and how he'd treated people in the past, their pain and deaths nothing to him, his emotions as hardened as his scarred heart.

To see someone else behaving in the same way had given him pause. In Jamaica he'd enjoyed dishing out punishments, hurting people; it had kept him from getting hurt himself. Who wanted to go into adulthood living the same life they had as a child, beaten and bruised, berated and made to feel like a piece of shit? He acted the way he did so no one would dare to treat him badly again, and for the first time in many years, he wished he'd taken a different path.

He sat next to a man called Jimmy at a large table upstairs and wondered whether George, sitting opposite, would lie to him like he'd lied to the other two. He'd told them if they said what he wanted to hear then they'd be banished from London, yet they were dead.

Another thing that Raffia had done himself. Made promises he hadn't kept. The power that surged through him afterwards, whenever people realised he'd duped them, it was like nothing else.

All the faces of the tourists he'd scammed had stayed in his mind, he hadn't forgotten a single one, and in the past that had served him well at night in his bed when he'd set up what amounted to an app in his head where he'd flip right and a new face appeared. He could remember how they'd looked at the point when they'd realised he was going to take their money compared to when he'd offered his services to show them the way. They'd been happy then, some of them, but others had been wary, especially Freya.

There was something about her he hated. Maybe the pity in her eyes when she'd first seen him was what had sewn the seeds of dislike. As if she thought she was better than him.

Everyone else got seated around the table with their cups of coffee from a machine over on the sideboard, Big B next to George, Greg on the other side of him. Moody came to sit on Raffia's right. He had the good sense to realise that if he didn't pull something miraculous out of the bag then he was going to meet the same fate as the two men downstairs whose bodies were rapidly cooling in the water, maybe a fish or two already coming up to investigate the infiltrators to their home. But there were tools on the table downstairs, and he shuddered at the thought of being so unlucky that they'd be used on him.

And why wouldn't he be unlucky, he always had been as a boy, treated unfairly by his father who'd whipped him with his belt. He could be whipped again within the hour, or he could be cut, strangled, so many things.

"Tell me a bit about your life," George said.

The scent of coffee was tormenting Raffia. He hadn't been given one, but Big B had. And wasn't that odd? Wasn't it fucking strange to give one of your soon-to-be victims a nice hot drink but not the other? Why did it feel like he was facing an inquisition, like in a board meeting, and Big B was one of the directors?

Fuck no, don't say he's on their side.

It wouldn't be the first time someone in the gang had deflected. They were still on the lookout for Cussing Cat who'd come over here to deal with one of the targets but hadn't returned. He likely lived under an assumed name in the UK, or maybe he'd gone elsewhere. The gang would never know because their reach didn't extend to being able to find out if someone's passport had been used.

Had Big B turned his back on them all?

"I... I grew up in Ocho Rios, haven't been anywhere else until I came here this week. I was an unwanted child and treated like shit, beaten, all that. When I joined the gang I belonged, I was wanted, and I got the family I never had."

"Tell them what a bastard you are, though," Big B said, confirming Raffia's fears.

He's been turned. Jesus.

"I did what I had to do," Raffia said. "To survive."

"But you did things you didn't need to." Big B went on to give a comprehensive list of Raffia's actions over the past few years.

They sounded so bad that even Raffia cringed. And this was it, he wasn't walking free, he wouldn't be banished. If the drowned men had been killed just for impersonating these twins, then Raffia didn't stand a chance now all of his sins hovered in the air between them.

He longed to rub his sore wrists, held together with cable ties. He knew the trick, the one that meant he could snap the tie, but with a man either side of him, wedging him in against the table, there was no chance he'd get away from them. He'd never make it to the door, but sitting here waiting for his fate to happen didn't seem right either. He didn't want to die, he just wanted to go home to the sea and the sand and the tourists. He didn't want to take his last breath on foreign soil.

"You sound like a right bastard," George said. "A bit like me, except you don't seem to have a heart when it matters. I used to come across like that, but I was lucky because my brother was always watching and always pulled me back when I was about to go too far. He taught me to let people go sometimes, or to be lenient, or to just give them a second smile or a bum knee like yours. I'm not horrible *all* the time, but it seems you've got a permanent chip on your shoulder, you haven't learned any humility. I'm not going to lie to you like I did to those other two, I'm going to give it to you straight. You *are* going to die, and the only thing that needs clearing up first is whether it's me or Big B who kills you."

Chapter Thirty-Six

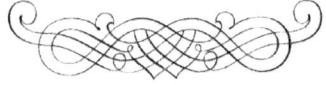

That was a completely unexpected statement, and Big B examined his feelings. Did he want to kill Raffia? At one time he would have, yes, he'd thought of it often enough in the dead of night and even under the bright-blue sky with the sun on his back and the scent of sun cream in the air, but he was turning over a new leaf, trying to become a better person, the person he was inside. He didn't want any blood on his hands going forward. As far as the gang were aware, Fish and Chips had killed Raffia, and if Big B did it then it would be written all over his face when he was questioned upon his return home. It was best he stayed out of it.

"What?" Raffia spat out.

Big B wasn't sure whether to feel sorry for him or not. Raffia had experienced many knocks in his life, but he'd taken them out on people, just like his father had done to him. He hadn't learned from the abuse but foisted it upon others, probably as some kind of power play or to make himself feel better. He hadn't had an epiphany where he'd chosen a better path, or if he had he'd ignored it and continued on the road to destruction.

No, I won't feel sorry for him.

"You do it," Big B said to George.

"Fine by me. I've got some anger to get out of me because of what those two dickheads did, pretending to be us, and even if I wasn't angry, I can dispatch him, no problem. I won't be having an attack of conscience with him, not after what he's done to those poor cows who did nothing but mind their own business while they were on holiday. He's a fucking bastard who doesn't deserve any mercy—like he didn't give any mercy to the people he treated like shit."

Some of the things Big B had told the people around this table were horrendous. Raffia had thought nothing about scarring people's faces, people who'd declined to become part of the gang. He'd gone after them in the middle of the night, crept in through their windows—or just the square hole in the wall if they didn't have glass. Many of them lived in run-down housing, their mothers making ends meet by selling fruit on the roadside, their fathers peddling weed, a side of Jamaican life that had been hidden from the holiday brochures.

Raffia stared across the table at Big B, his eyes narrowed, as though he still had power over him, and the weird thing was that he did. He still had the ability to flip Big B's stomach over.

But I have to remind myself that my life might change now.

It hadn't gone unnoticed that he'd been given coffee and Raffia hadn't. Was there a chance he'd be allowed to go home? Should he dare hope that George's gesture of handing him a cup was his way of saying he could go free? Regardless, Big B had spilled the beans on Raffia anyway, an extra push on letting the twins know he was on their side and not his. He had to do this for his mother and sister, and for himself. He deserved to live a life outside of the gang.

In an indication that he hoped would let Raffia know exactly where he was in the pecking order, Big B raised his coffee cup. "Cheers."

Chapter Thirty-Seven

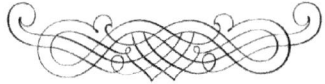

George had put a forensic suit on, the hood up, shoe covers over his trainers, and goggles protecting his eyes. He was covered in blood. Greg had hauled the dead unidentical twins up so George could use the electric saw to chop their bodies into pieces while Raffia stood and watched, Jimmy on one side, Moody on the other, holding him steady. A couple of times Raffia's legs had given way, and he'd hung in their grip, vomiting on the floor as bits of flesh were cut off. George had used a long-handled squeegee and swept the sick into the water as if Raffia hadn't been having the worst time of his life so far.

But the worst was yet to come.

People could act like they were hard and had a strong stomach, but when they were actually presented with something that would test their mettle, they generally failed, unless they'd been exposed to such a thing over and over again to the point that it became normal. Boring, even. Raffia had clearly not been overly exposed to bodies being sliced, but then who would be unless they worked for George and Greg or other outfits that behaved in the same way?

With the blood mopped up by Greg using bleach water, the trapdoor closed, and Raffia now held up with one set of chains, it was time for round two. Jimmy and Moody had gone upstairs for a shower and a change of clothes. Greg stood next to Big B by the chain crank. George positioned himself in front of a naked Raffia, his skinny body pitiful to see, his ribs showing through his skin, resembling a fishing creel.

"Didn't you earn enough in the gang to feed your-fucking-self?" George asked.

Raffia didn't answer.

"Where did your money go, because it's obvious you didn't get your hair done properly and you didn't buy nice clothes. According to Freya you looked like a fucking tramp when you walked up to her at the front of the resort."

No answer.

"It's obvious you're not going to talk, and to be honest with you, I can't be bothered anyway. We've been awake for hours on end, and this little job needs to come to a close. Or this part of the job, I should say. Before you go and meet your maker, though, I'll let you know what's what. Chubby Chandler thinks you're already dead, by the way, that was dealt with while you were asleep on the journey here. Fish and Chips slit your throat, took the money, and also took Freya. That's the story that Big B's going with when he goes home. He'll be taking some money with him to hand over to someone who can get his name changed, and that of his sister and mother, and they're going to live a good life, something he's wanted to do for a long time. In order to get that, he's chosen to take down the whole gang, except it won't be him doing it, per se, but the police. Once he's settled in Kingston or wherever else he chooses to go, we'll be passing on all the information we have to the British police, who'll then go and give the UK Jamaican contacts a little visit. No more selling British tourists. No more tourists being terrorised while they're on holiday. I think that's called a job well done, don't you, my old son?"

George lashed out with a whip fitted with treble hooks used for fishing that bit into Raffia's skin and ripped it this way and that, exposing raw, red flesh, blood seeping, pouring in places where the barbs had burrowed deep. Raffia screamed, but George tuned him out, immersing himself in the glory of the kill, slashing and slashing until no part of the man's skin was left unscathed. He dropped the whip to the floor behind him and selected one of his mediaeval tools, securing it around Raffia's wedding tackle and twisting the screw so the contraption's teeth bit into the base of the cock and balls, squeezing and squeezing until Raffia passed out.

That was quick.

George abandoned that task, it was pointless continuing to screw if he couldn't hear the effect it was having, and took a moment to watch the blood dripping from Raffia's groin area, meandering down his inner thighs over the ragged flesh and mixing with the other blood already there. Greg opened the trapdoor, the blood now dripping into the water, then he went back to stand with Big B who looked decidedly ill.

"You don't have to witness this, you know," George said to him. "Go upstairs if it makes you feel uncomfortable. Talk to Moody or Jimmy if you need to."

Big B lumbered away upstairs—he'd passed George's final test: he couldn't stomach standing there watching Raffia die, and added to him informing them of Raffia's misdemeanours in Jamaica, Big B really did just want to start life anew.

"So, it's just you and me, bruv," George said to Greg. "You take the right side and I take the left?"

Greg nodded and fired up the second electric saw, and together they sliced through a body that harboured the soul of a spiteful and nasty man, one who'd got lucky and wouldn't get to feel the pain of his death, but if such a place as Hell existed, then George could only hope that the Jamaican burned there for all eternity.

Wanker.

Chapter Thirty-Eight

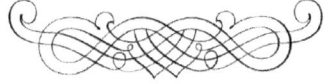

Freya hadn't slept too well, which wasn't surprising, considering everything that had been going on, but Puggy had slept even worse, and she'd ended up sitting against the wall on his bed, his hand in hers, while they'd talked in between brief dozes that flung her into nightmare territory every time.

Puggy had told her about his dream of owning every single pair of trainers Nike had ever created. And he was desperate to get back to classes at the community centre, as he'd only had one and was having a serious case of FOMO. He promised her he wouldn't let anyone else take advantage of him again and just receive the money from the twins when he passed them messages. No more taking on extra jobs for pocket money. Maybe his new friend, Sarah, would help him to fill his time.

George and Greg had arrived at the safe house. They'd all gathered around the kitchen table, food from a sandwich shop spread out in front of them and coffee in takeaway cups. Will had gone off somewhere, clearly used to making himself scarce once the bosses had shown up. He'd been brilliant, such a nice and kind person, putting their minds at rest last night when darkness had fallen and things had seemed that little bit more sinister. They'd played card games, and Puggy had really enjoyed that, seeming to forget everything for a while until he'd taken in their surroundings again and remembered why they were there. It was so obvious he was afraid of Fish and Chips, more so Fish, and Freya hoped the twins had done something about them so they would definitely leave Puggy alone now.

He currently ate a cheese and ham baguette, having taken the lid off his coffee so it wasn't too hot for him to drink. He seemed so childlike in some ways and yet clever in others, and she'd established from what he'd told her that he was on the spectrum but not what else he suffered with. He'd mentioned having to go to physio recently, and she'd wondered whether he had muscle problems. She hadn't pried, preferring that he tell her himself whenever he was ready. Depending on what happened next would determine whether she saw him again. She hoped so, but at the same time if it meant she needed to keep herself safe and move away, then that's what she'd have to do.

"Right, here's the deal," George said. "Freya, you can either stay in one of our flats and arrange with your employer to work from home for a while until we know what's going on in Jamaica regarding the gang, or you can have a new name and start again elsewhere."

She'd already given this some thought, and London would never feel safe to her now, not since she'd been abducted from her own home. In her line of work she could go freelance, she had a pick of customers she could poach, introducing herself as though she was someone they didn't know, and they could pay her through PayPal using an email address in her new name. Maybe starting again somewhere else was for the best. Mum might even come with her. Freya would miss Lottie, but going through what she had had taught her that feeling safe and secure was the most important thing to her. She had to move forward in order to get herself on the road to recovery. Standing still and moping about what had gone on wasn't going to help her.

"I'll go to Liverpool."

"While we get things sorted for you, sourcing you somewhere to live up there or whatever, you can stay here. We'll get you a new phone so you can chat to your mum."

"Thank you. What happened to Big B?"

George gave Puggy a quick glance to likely let her know he wasn't prepared to discuss that in front of him, and rightly so, she should never have brought the subject up when she knew Puggy could get upset the way he did. Guilt brought a flush of heat to her cheeks and tears to her eyes. Puggy seemed oblivious to her distress, though, and when Greg asked him if he'd like to go outside with his food and eat it in the garden in the sun with him, he smiled and left the room.

The kitchen door closed, and Freya wiped the tears. "Sorry, I didn't think."

"It's fine, he didn't pick up on anything. I'll tell him that Fish and Chips have moved away and they won't be bothering him again. As for Big B, he's on a plane at the minute, going back to Jamaica." George explained the deal there, nodding to himself as though acknowledging that he'd made the right decision in letting him go.

As far as Freya was concerned, Big B was her hero regardless of what he'd done in the past. What mattered was that he'd come forward and basically saved her. He'd tried to make her feel less scared during the abduction, and she should hate him for even being part of the kidnap, but it had been clear even then that he was a good man underneath it all and was doing things under duress.

She felt bad for thinking that he wouldn't stick to his promise in trying to free her, because he had, and now his life might be in danger.

"And Raffia…" George said.

Now there was a man she didn't want to be set free. The way he'd made her feel when he'd forced her to hand over the money in Jamaica, she'd never forget it, nor would she forget seeing his horrible eyes through the letterbox slot at Puggy's flat. She didn't like to hate anyone, but she hated him, and she hated herself for hating him because that wasn't the type of person she was. God, she hadn't even hated James for what he'd done, ripping her life apart, all for a bit of emotional backup from some woman at work.

Something he could have got from me.

Don't go there. That's over, gone, there are worse memories to tackle now.

"Is he dead?" she asked.

"Yes. Do you want to know how it went?"

Did she?

"It depends how bad it was."

"Very."

"Then no. But did it hurt?"

"Quite a bit."

"Good." And that was alien to her, too, getting satisfaction from someone else's pain, but what about the pain *he'd* caused *her*? She wasn't about to feel sorry for him. She had a new life to begin, one thrust upon her because she was too afraid to stay in London now, and besides, she didn't want to risk bumping into James.

It was best to walk away and start again.

Chapter Thirty-Nine

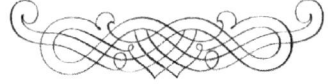

The plane landed in Montego Bay with a couple of jolts of the wheels and a round of applause from the passengers. Tears burned Maven's eyes—he wouldn't be Big B again until his meeting with Chubby Chandler and Digby Dog. The relief that he was home was so immense that a lump filled his throat. A few times in

London he hadn't thought he'd make it here, that he'd die in that cellar, but he'd been gifted a reprieve and the money to start a brand-new life, and he wasn't going to squander it.

He loved the irony that the money George had given him had originated from the gang.

While he was desperate to get off the plane, go through the airport protocols, and find the bus bound for Ocho Rios, he remained in his seat, too tired to fight his way into the long line of people tugging hand luggage from the overhead compartments. It took a while for everyone to disembark, but then it was his turn. He took his rucksack and made his way down the aisle, leaving the plane via the air bridge. Humidity smacked him in the face almost as soon as he'd walked a few paces into the airport, and he could cry again at how it felt like home, sweat breaking out all over him already.

It wasn't long before he stood outside in the heat, the scent of Jamaica all around him as well as the chatter of holidaymakers heading for their coaches that would take them to various resorts. Ocho Rios was a couple of hours away, but he'd sleep on the bus, catching up on the lack of rest he'd had the night before.

Placing his backpack straps over his shoulders, he changed his mind about a bus and instead opted for a taxi. He had a lot of money on him, just under the allowed airport allowance of ten thousand US dollars in cash, so it wouldn't hurt to splurge. He got in the first cab in the line, holding out three hundred up front so the driver knew he was good for it. He took his backpack off and sat in the back, his way of saying he didn't want to talk. The car set off, and he watched the familiar landscape rolling by.

His mind drifted to the meeting he was going to have later, going through the supposed actions of Fish and Chips and finding out whether the UK Jamaican man had been informed that his so-called trusted contacts had shafted everyone. He had no idea whether that contact was going to be visited by the twins, and it was probably best he didn't. The less he knew, the less he had to feel guilty about.

After the meeting, he'd go and speak to Cheap Fred who'd know who he should contact regarding a name change. Cheap Fred knew a lot of people and was trustworthy, always had been as far as Maven was concerned—and it helped that the man was his father. Although estranged from Maven's mother some years back, Cheap Fred had done his best to look after Maven, but Sharina didn't want anything to do with him. Maven wasn't about to tell his mother and sister who'd helped them disappear in Kingston; they wouldn't want to receive Cheap Fred's help, so that was going to have to be a secret between father and son.

Then there was the task of telling his mother and Sharina that they all had to leave for their own safety, and he'd have to confess who he'd been and what he'd done, and show them the money, more than his mother had ever thought she'd see in her lifetime, and they'd leave in the darkness, beginning again in a small apartment Cheap Fred would likely get for them.

Soon Maven would be living an anonymous life, as close to the beach as he could get. He couldn't ask for any more than that.

Chapter Forty

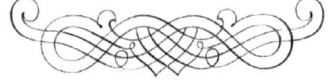

Sharon sat in a café, only it wasn't the one round the corner from her old flat. To anyone who asked, she owned the gaff, other people employed to sort out the deliveries and making the food and doing everything else associated with running a business. Sharon didn't have a fucking clue, see. She was just there to listen and watch, getting pally with the customers. A few had even gone so far as to ask her to sit down with them for a cuppa, and she'd obliged, waiting for a tidbit she could pass on to the twins.

The Shiny Fork was one of their new fronts, and in a hidden partition behind a wall out the back in the storeroom was a stash of something she didn't want to know about. She'd never been tempted to look in the boxes—besides, they were sealed with brown tape, and it would be obvious if she peeled it back; they'd know she'd been snooping, and she didn't want to give them any cause to sack her and take her nice new flat away.

The kids had settled in so well, but at first, despite being happy they had rooms of their own—one done out in red, the other blue—one of them would inevitably crawl into the bed of the other, maybe missing the closeness of having someone nearby in the same room, or it could even be missing the sound of someone else's breathing. They'd grow out of it eventually, and they were still so young that it didn't matter.

She spent a lot of her time in the Shiny Fork wiping tables and generally tidying up; that way she looked innocent and like she couldn't possibly be listening to any conversations. She got a little full-body thrill whenever somebody said something she thought the twins might need to know, but she'd never heard any feedback about what had happened to anyone after she'd passed on the snippets.

Maybe it was best she didn't know. If she did, then she might feel bad that she'd been the one to bring about somebody's downfall.

She went to the window to give the large, deep sill a wipe, moving a couple of display baskets, one containing fake bread and the other plastic lemons. She glanced across the street, frowning at two men in suits who appeared to be arguing outside Home Bargains. One of them took a hand from his pocket, thrusting his fist towards the other man's stomach, then he turned and ran off, darting down an alley beside Superdrug.

The stabbed man bent his head to look down. Blood coated his white shirt. People gave him a wide berth, but someone else rushed forward to perhaps ask if he wanted some help.

Sharon briefly turned away from the window to look at her customers. No one seemed to have noticed the commotion outside, nor that she'd witnessed it. What a relief, it meant when the police came calling to ask questions, she could say she hadn't seen a thing. There wasn't any CCTV on the opposite buildings pointing at her precious little establishment, so everything would be fine.

What wasn't fine was the stabbed man. Not that he'd been stabbed, she couldn't care less about that, but she cared about why he was here. A ghost from her past who'd reared his very ugly head. She risked a glance back outside as she straightened the basket of bread. He stared right at her, seeming alarmed that she'd spotted him watching, then he staggered off down the street, clutching his stomach, a policeman getting out of a patrol car and running after him.

It could all kick off now. Her new, perfect life could be ruined.

But not if she could help it.

She took her cleaning cloth and spray out into the back, going into her office and shutting the door. She took an ancient burner phone from the locked drawer in the desk and brought up the only contact in the list.

Seven. He'd know what to do.

She sent a message, the one they'd agreed on if either of them ever encountered people from their past.

Mayday!

It could be a while before he responded. If he was anything like her he'd have his secret phone switched off for the majority of the time, too.

There was nothing she could do now but wait.

To be continued in *Refurb*,
the *Cardigan Estate* 42

Printed in Dunstable, United Kingdom

63793044R00224